GAVIN

The Mavericks, Book 11

Dale Mayer

Books in This Series:

GAVIN: THE MAVERICKS, BOOK 11
Dale Mayer
Valley Publishing Ltd.

ISBN-13: 978-1-773363-03-5
Print Edition

About This Book

What happens when the very men—trained to make the hard decisions—come up against the rules and regulations that hold them back from doing what needs to be done? They either stay and work within the constraints given to them or they walk away. Only now, for a select few, they have another option:

The Mavericks. A covert black ops team that steps up and break all the rules ... but gets the job done.

Welcome to a new military romance series by *USA Today* best-selling author Dale Mayer. A series where you meet new friends and just might get to meet old ones too in this raw and compelling look at the men who keep us safe every day from the darkness where they operate—and live—in the shadows ... until someone special helps them step into the light.

When four members of one family-owned corporation are kidnapped off the streets in Honolulu, Gavin's intel says this is a corporate espionage case ... but is it?

There's not much to like about this case. Too many people are involved, ... including an old friend of Gavin's. But, as Gavin digs deeper into the motives of the suspect pool, events get uglier, and bodies start to fall.

Rosalina has no idea how she ended up in this nightmare, but all she cares about is her ailing parents who have been separated from her and her sister. Even when she and her sister are freed, Rosalina finds no sign of their mother or father. Trying to rescue them means deciphering friend from foe ...

It comes down to the wire as this close family corporation falls apart, revealing the core of darkness inside, ... and leaves Gavin and Rosalina struggling to stay safe as enemies work to take out them both.

PROLOGUE

"ARE YOU SURE I can't look now?" Helena complained good-naturedly, her eyes shut.

"No," Gavin said. "You don't get to look at anything right now."

"That's not fair," she said. Gavin had her in the passenger side of his Jeep. They were heading to Lennox's, and Lennox and Carolina were expecting them.

"And we would have been here a long time ago," Gavin said, "but you're the one who wanted to stop and get flowers."

"Of course I did!" she said, as her arms tightened around the big bouquet. "It's my first visit to Lennox's house."

"Hardly a visit," he said. "You're moving in."

"I am," she said, a blissful smile on her face.

Lennox was, indeed, a lucky man, Gavin thought. He didn't know how the hell these two had finally gotten past their differences, but they had, and that's what counted. And now here Gavin was, taking her to Lennox's house, while she took her first step into their future. Gavin pulled up to the front, parked, and said, "Now I'm coming around to your side."

"Okay, okay," but she hopped out impatiently and waited for him to grab her arm. As they got to the sidewalk, he said, "Now you can open your eyes."

1

She looked up to see the stone-and-cedar Tudor house in front of them for her very first time, one that Gavin had seen many times. "Oh, my goodness," she said, "it's gorgeous."

The door opened, and Lennox stepped out. She cried out, handed off the flowers to Gavin right before she raced forward. Lennox opened his arms, and she dashed into them. Lennox picked her up and swung her around in his arms.

Gavin stood back and smiled up at them. "You two look perfect together," he declared.

"Good," Lennox said. "It's taken Carolina and me a couple days to get everything ready."

Gavin nodded. His phone went off just then. "Hang on. I'll be there in a minute."

"Don't bother," Lennox said. "I can tell you all about it."

He looked at his phone and back at his buddy and asked, "What is it?"

"The next job," Lennox said. "I've got your orders here. I was going to hand them to you before the call came through, but you guys were late."

Gavin laughed. "Am I going alone?"

"No," Lennox said, "you're going with a friend. You just don't know which one."

"And you?"

"I'm running ground crew," Lennox said with a grin. "I get to stay here with my beautiful Helena."

"Okay, that'll be pretty sucky on my part but perfect for you. Do I get to come inside for a bit before I head out?"

"Sorry, bud."

Just then a military vehicle pulled up to the front of the house.

Lennox held out a brown envelope to Gavin and then pointed. "That's your ride."

"What about my gear?"

"It's all waiting for you." Lennox turned Helena around and said, "Say goodbye to Gavin."

She lifted a hand, confusion on her face.

Gavin smiled and said, "I'll be back."

"We'll wait for you," she said.

He shook his head. "Don't bother. I won't be back for days yet. Have a good one." And he hopped into the truck and headed off. He had the brown envelope from Lennox, but that's all he had. He looked at the driver and asked, "What are your orders?"

"I'm taking you to the dock," he said. "A destroyer's waiting for you."

"Any other details?"

"None," he said.

"Fine, let's go." Gavin was headed somewhere; he just didn't know where yet. And maybe that was okay too.

CHAPTER 1

G AVIN WERKSTER DROPPED his duffel bag on the bottom bunk before jumping up to the top, where he laid down to open the envelope Lennox had given him. The trip from Lennox's house to the docks and out to the USS *Gettysburg* had been fast and furious, but he was here now, and he still had no clue where he was going or what he was doing.

Before he had a chance to even open the envelope and dump out the contents, the door opened, and a man walked in and did the exact same thing Gavin did. His duffel bag hit the bottom bunk, and he jumped up onto the top bunk opposite Gavin. Then he rolled over, looked at him, and said, "What the hell, Gavin. You want to explain why I'm here?"

Gavin's jaw dropped. "Shane?"

His old buddy grinned somewhat sheepishly. "Yeah. It's me. Not exactly sure why I'm here or even how."

"Well, unless they shanghaied you somewhere," Gavin said, "you probably have about as much understanding of what's going on as I did before the last job."

"You helped out Lennox, correct?" Shane asked.

"Yep," Gavin said. "So you know Lennox?"

"I did a tour with him, yes. But I haven't seen you in what, three years?"

"At least that," Gavin said, as he sat up and reached across, and the two men did a forearm shake across the aisle. "Damn good to see you."

"It is," Shane said cheerfully.

That was the thing about this guy. He always had a positive and optimistic attitude; in fact, sometimes he was too damn cheery. But Gavin had always appreciated it, since some guys were such serious downers. But not Shane. He was a fun guy to have around. "Do you have any clue what's going on?"

"Not much," Shane said. "Lennox told me that you had the deets." He motioned to the envelope Gavin had in front of him. "So what are we doing?"

"A businessman and his wife have been kidnapped, apparently. That's as far as I'd gotten." He sat up straighter, and, grabbing the envelope, he said, "Let's take a look." He pulled out several stacks of paper, took half of it, and handed the rest of it off to Shane. "When I worked with Lennox, I had more details than he did."

"A file was supposed to come with me," Shane said, "but it didn't make it."

"Paper copy?"

"A USB," he said. "So Lennox told me to just talk to you."

"Great," he said. He pulled out his phone and quickly sent Lennox a text. **Shane's here. But he didn't come with anything.**

He came with enough, Lennox replied. **Check your phone. I'm uploading information.**

Gavin watched his phone downloading every link as it came through, since he didn't know when they would lose internet. At the same time he kept looking through the physical file. Most of it was background information into the family members, but no red flags popped at Gavin's cursory review. So the paper intel was bulky but provided little to pursue.

"So the businessman, his wife, and two daughters were on a trip through Japan," Gavin continued, as he shared what bits he knew with Shane. "They moved on from Japan to Hawaii."

"Sure, that makes sense," Shane said. "And then what?"

"Then they dropped off the face of the earth," Gavin said. "Last-known sighting was at the Marriott in Honolulu."

"Well, it would be pretty easy to disappear in that crowd," Shane said. "Talk about a major tourist draw."

"Exactly." Gavin nodded. "The question is, did they disappear willingly or were they 'disappeared' by somebody else?"

Shane cracked up at that. "Well, chances are it wasn't by choice," he said. "Do we have a clue where we're going?"

Gavin went on. "I presume we're heading toward Hawaii, but who the hell knows. They went missing two hours ago." He stopped and shook his head. "No way."

"No way what?"

"Seems like the report of them going missing coincides with the kidnapping event. How did we get that intel so fast? I'm not seeing anything about that in this packet." Reaching for his phone, Gavin quickly sent a text asking Lennox. The reply message came back immediately.

Daughter called 9-1-1, and they could hear her screams on the phone.

So why the hell haven't you got somebody local there?

We do, Lennox texted. **Don't get comfy.**

Gavin snorted at that. **Great. I'm already what, seventy miles from the coast?**

Yep, you are. Flights will be picking you up pretty quick too.

Not even time for coffee?

Hell no.

Gavin stared at that and shook his head, but then he got a knock on the door. Immediately the two men hopped from their bunks, grabbed their bags, and collected the paperwork from the file that they still hadn't had a chance to read fully. They followed the seaman at the door. Still trying to download as much of the material as Gavin could onto his phone, he and Shane continued up to the deck, where the helicopter awaited them. They were quickly loaded and immediately took off out over the water. Gavin sent one message to Lennox. **In the air.**

For this leg, yes, Lennox replied.

Gavin shook his head and pocketed his phone. Looking at Shane, he said, "If nothing else, the methods of travel are pretty interesting."

"Anything but commercial works for me," Shane said. "I'm too big for those damn tiny airplane seats."

As he said it, Gavin eyed Shane's 250-pound frame with broader shoulders than his own. "Haven't ever considered what a commercial flight would be like for you."

"Absolute hell, that's what," he said. "Absolute hell. But, hey, I've done it before, and I'll do it again."

"Good to know," Gavin said, "because, in this business, it seems like it's nothing but craziness."

"Exactly." Shane resumed looking through the material and said, "So the father was there for a business meeting on medical implants and prosthetics. He's a doctor, a researcher, and a scientist. Looks like his wife works with him in the same field." Shane continued to read out loud their biographies. "Both are in their sixties with two adult daughters. One is missing a leg and wears a prosthetic, which started them down this path. The other one is a scientist and a doctor and a researcher in her own right," Shane said, with an eyebrow raised.

"More brainy people," Gavin noted, as he studied the water under them. "What the hell is going on in the world that all the brainiacs keep getting into trouble?"

"The problem is," Shane said, "that other people want use of their brains."

"Good point," Gavin said, as he looked at the images in his part of the physical file. "Standard gray-haired male professor and matching wife," he said. "Nothing very distinguishable about either of them."

"Nope. The one daughter appears to be twenty-two, no, forty-two, sorry. She's divorced with two children and went on this as part of a family trip. Her fiancé and children are in Honolulu and are safe."

Gavin frowned. "Interesting that the four of them were taken but not the extended family."

"Wrong place at the wrong time, maybe," Shane wondered.

"Yeah." Gavin's gaze fell on the image of the other daughter. "So, the second daughter looks quite a bit younger."

"Thirty-one," Shane read off his stat sheet. "Scientist in her own right and also working in the family business."

"But not the daughter who's missing a leg?"

"No. Not from what I've got here anyway."

"She's also very striking," Gavin said.

"Yeah, nobody'll miss seeing her walk down the street."

"Beauty and brains," Gavin said. He faced Shane. "We've had several cases where those two were combined already."

"So, in this case, was she the target, and everybody else was collateral damage, or were the parents the intended targets? They own a significant interest in Trident Corporation. Like 33 percent of the shares, technically 16.5 percent for each of the parents."

"Anybody own 51 percent?" Gavin asked.

"Just checking," Shane replied, and then he whistled. "Each of the daughters owns 10 percent as well, giving the immediate family a controlling interest."

"Well then, 53 percent of the company. The major shareholders."

"Not exactly," he said. "The rest, the 47 percent, is in a family trust, granted by the paternal grandfather. With funds not to be released until two years after his passing."

"Is that normal?"

Shane gave a one-arm shrug. "I wonder if this could be more of a business play."

"Hard to say," Gavin replied. "For all we know, somebody just knows they have lots of money, and it's a simple ransom deal."

"Who would pay it if the entire family is kidnapped? Do they have other grandparents still alive? Siblings?"

"I'll ask for more data," Gavin said.

Shane asked, "I understand there's a chat system too?"

"Yes. But I'll give you a number, and you can text into that." Gavin quickly gave him the number he used for information gathering. "Just be aware that whatever you ask for tends to come."

Shane looked up, an eyebrow raised. "So, like a whiskey at ten o'clock for a nightcap?"

"If they can get it to you, they will," Gavin said, in all seriousness. "So we try not to waste it on trivialities."

"Message received," Shane said. "But since when is a nightcap trivial?"

Gavin shook his head, but he couldn't tear his gaze from the image of the beautiful woman in front of him. She wore a white lab coat, and her arms were crossed over her chest, as if impatient for someone to take the picture so she could move on. Instead of a flirtatious look in her eyes, he saw more of an intelligence, questioning the wisdom behind wasting five minutes of her time to do this photo op. Or maybe it was just her reaction when someone took her photo. He shook his head. "There's a definite tilt to her jaw that means she's not the easiest to deal with."

"Who?" Shane asked, looking up. But then he caught Gavin staring at the image.

"Her name is Rosalina Rennert," he said.

Gavin continued to go through the paperwork until he understood exactly what had happened in Honolulu. But, regardless of the stacks of paperwork he had been given in the envelope, the relevant information was very slim. The family had gone out for dinner, and, on the way back to the hotel, all four had been shanghaied into a van.

The hotel security cameras had picked up the actual occurrence and had tracked the license plate, but the vehicle itself had been ditched a few blocks away, and they'd switched to a different vehicle with no license plates. Gavin suspected, very soon afterward, that vehicle had probably been ditched as well. In other words somebody was moving and moving quickly and efficiently.

"Well, I don't have a problem going to Hawaii," Gavin said, "but I would like to know the motive behind this kidnapping before I get there."

"We should be there within twelve hours of when they were snatched," Shane said, "and the Mavericks at command central are collecting as much information as they can get for us."

"Twelve hours is too long," Gavin chafed.

"Maybe," Shane said, "but we're moving as fast as we can."

And, sure enough, they landed on another carrier and were moved to another helicopter. They pretty well were hopscotching their way from one to another. "We should be in Hawaii sooner than we expected," Gavin said, looking at his watch.

"We've cut off a good two hours from a commercial airline flight," Shane said. "Interesting mode of travel."

"Yeah, just missing the food," Gavin said. "As soon as we land, we'll need a place to stay and food at some point."

"The paperwork states we've got accommodations in the same Marriott. Plus we have a liaison set up with local police—someone from one of the military bases is waiting for us," Shane said, frowning. "They'll be attached to our mission."

"I don't like that," Gavin said, as he stared at Shane, shaking his head. "Okay, the additional download is complete, or I just lost internet service. Let's get through the paperwork first, share any usable intel. Then one of us can sleep for two or three hours while the other reviews the data on my phone. Then we'll switch up, compare notes. See what leads we can find to pursue once we're on the ground."

THERE APPROACHED THE Oahu airport, off to the side where the private planes were. A large helicopter hangar was here as well. Gavin hopped out as soon as he could, then bent down and walked away from the helicopter.

"I don't think we're supposed to go in this direction," Shane called out.

"I don't give a shit," Gavin said. He was a part of the Mavericks for a reason. No more ridiculous red-tape rules that made no sense. He enjoyed avoiding all that and getting down to work. Plus he appreciated his Maverick buddies, and they hadn't been working with anybody else so far, and Gavin didn't plan on signing up for that extra baggage to restrict him now. "Nobody attaches themselves to us or to our mission, much less dictates what we do."

He could feel Shane's surprise. Looking at his buddy, he said, "I just want to make sure that we're free and clear to do what we need to do," he said. "I can't operate effectively with someone trying to tie my hands all the time."

"They said you'd be difficult," a voice called out.

Gavin turned to look, his eyebrows going up. "Steve?"

The man walked toward him with a lazy grin on his face, his hand outstretched to shake. The two men shook hands as Gavin introduced him to Shane.

"Steve Arbrey, what are you doing here?" Gavin asked.

"Whatever I need to," he said. "I was told to meet you and to take you to your hotel first off."

"Why can't we go on our own?" he asked.

"Because I'll debrief you," Steve said, sounding exasperated. "You're still the same go-go Gavin, aren't you?"

Gavin shrugged. "Well, we've got a whole family missing," he said, "and it doesn't seem like taking our time is a very good option. We're almost halfway into those first critical twenty-four hours."

"Which is why I'm debriefing you on the way," he said, as he pointed out a black SUV ahead of him. "Come on. Let's go." As they hopped into the vehicle, Gavin looked around and asked, "Why you?"

"Because Melinda is my fiancée," he said. "And I damn well want to get her back alive and well."

"Interesting," Gavin said. "You know the military likes to keep you guys a hell of a long way away from any personal involvement in an investigation."

"Yes," he said, "but I asked to drive you in so I could talk to you and to give you some personals about the family."

"Well then, let's hear it," Gavin said and put his phone on Record.

"The two daughters were raised almost as if separate families," he said. "Melinda is early forties, Rosalina is early thirties. With a decade between them, the sisters didn't have a whole lot to do with each other. There were a lot of problems and jealousy until they became adults and came together, working on a common goal, which is working for the company."

"Problems in the company?"

"No. Not that I know of."

"Either of them angling to take over the company?"

"No. Not that I know of."

"Do you have shares in the company?"

"No," he said, "but obviously Melinda does."

"Yes. Each sister has 10 percent according to our intel," Shane added.

"What are the board members like?" Gavin asked.

"Stuffy old white men," Steve said. Then he laughed. "That's according to Melinda."

"Right, and how long have you known her?"

"Five years," he said. "My brother was on a mission in Afghanistan and got his foot blown off. I met her through his treatments and the process of getting back on his feet with some state-of-the-art technology. He was part of a military program, testing out new stuff for Melinda's company."

"So Trident has defense contracts?"

"No, they have military contracts," he corrected. "Nothing defense-related about it."

"Ah," Gavin said. "Interesting. So keep talking. What do we need to know?"

Steve filled him in on what he knew about the family, but it was all cursory boyfriend and peripheral stuff.

"Enemies?"

"Not that I know of."

"Corporate enemies?"

At that, Steve shrugged. "A couple competing companies, sure."

"Anybody competing for the same contract?"

"Not that I know of."

"We need to find out," Gavin said, looking at Shane, who was busy texting and sending messages. He nodded at his partner, then turned to Steve again. "Does anybody have a line on the men who grabbed them off the street?"

"No. We initially thought it might have been a terrorist group. But nobody's recognized them."

"Ransom note?"

"Nothing," he said. "And no one has claimed responsibility either."

"Which a terrorist group definitely would have. But, in this case, we'd also have bodies to show for it," Shane chimed in.

"So, a private problem then?" Gavin asked Steve.

"It's possible. The father has a brother, and the mother has two sisters. They're all friendly enough. I can't see anybody kidnapping them over something personal."

"So, you are the fiancé of the one woman, but what about the other woman, Rosalina?" Gavin asked. "What about her relationships?"

"She was married to a doctor for a couple years. They divorced. She's been single ever since," Steve replied.

"Amicably divorced?"

"I believe so," he said. "The ex-husband remarried and has a two-year-old."

"So not still longing for her?"

"No. The divorce itself was a bit difficult, as I think all divorces are wont to be, but there didn't appear to be any lasting impact."

"Interesting," Gavin said. "Are they designing anything new? Anything different or unique? Do they have a million patents pending on something that the world really wants and that people are trying to get their hands on?"

"Not a million, but they do have over a dozen patents pending," Steve confirmed.

"That's fairly standard for any R&D company," Gavin said.

"They don't believe corporate espionage or anything along those lines is a part of this," Steve told them.

"*They?*" Gavin pounced. "Who is *they?*"

"The police," Steve said. "I'm in contact with them because I'm related, of course, as Melinda's fiancé." With that, his voice dropped. "Jesus Christ, I hope you can find them."

"We'll find them," Gavin promised, with a long exhale. "I just can't guarantee what shape they'll be in."

ROSALINA RENNERT WOKE up and looked around the small room she was in. She was seated on a chair, her hands tied behind her back, and both her feet were tied to one leg of the chair. Her sister faced her from across the table. The two of them stared at each other, wide-eyed and terrified. No sign of their parents. Rosalina wasn't gagged; her sister was.

"I have no clue what's going on here," Rosalina whispered. "Do you?"

Her sister shook her head emphatically.

"Have you been threatened or blackmailed?"

Her sister shook her head again.

Rosalina closed her eyes, trying to think. She knew she had a lot of brainpower, but this kind of stuff was beyond her. She did much better with numbers, equations, formulas. Human machinations and betrayal were beyond her ability to comprehend. She liked things simple and clear-cut. Not this bullshit.

If the kidnappers had wanted something from them, why hadn't they just said so? Instead, the two of them were sitting in this room for hours now. Her parents' safety worried her the most. They were older, and her dad already had a bit of a sticky ticker. Not good. Stress was something he was told to avoid.

That was a joke. This trip to Hawaii was supposed to be a chance for the family to reconnect after the diagnosis on his heart condition. Her father, being a little bit more solemn these days, had decided it was time to cut back. And look what happened. They all decided to cut back and to take a holiday to bond as a family; instead Melinda had been separated from her fiancé and her children, kidnapped along with Rosalina and their parents.

At least their parents had each other, assuming they were even together.

This room was more like a detention center, with cement walls, a table, and a single door. No windows at all. She expected a two-way mirror, but there wasn't even that.

They had barely arrived in Hawaii and had just started to destress and to spend some time with each other. Rosalina hadn't really ever connected with Melinda's kids before, so this was a chance to do that. They were from her previous marriage, though their father hadn't been in their lives for a couple years now. Rosalina really liked Melinda's fiancé, Steve, and was happy for her sister and proud of her for starting all over again. It was a really shitty time for something like this kidnapping to happen. *But when would be a good time for a kidnapping, right?* Though Melinda and Steve had been a couple for five years, they had just recently gotten engaged. Talk about a new beginning getting blown up in their faces.

"Did you recognize anybody?" she asked Melinda.

Again Melinda shook her head.

Rosalina wondered why she hadn't been gagged, yet Melinda had been. No point in asking, as her sister could only nod or shake her head.

Studying the ties on her ankles, Rosalina noted they were zap straps or zip ties but slightly different. They were effective, and it would be hard to get free, short of cutting them. So she wasn't going anywhere. She could jump and bounce her chair to maybe free her bound feet from the chair leg, but, even so, the door was probably locked anyway. Groaning, she glanced around and said, "A window would be nice."

Just the sound of her own voice was helpful, but it wasn't that helpful. She twisted her hands behind her, noting they were tied together but not tied to the chair. To get free, she realized that she could stand and slide her hands up over the back of the chair, but that wouldn't help much. Her hands remained tied behind her. She could get them under her butt, in theory, but, with both her legs tied to one of the chair legs, that additional maneuver wouldn't help her further.

Then she stared at her legs tied to the one chair leg and laughed. Now that she had her hands behind her back, she sat on her palms immediately and slid them through to the back of her knees, and then, in a swift movement, dumped her and her chair backward, then slid her feet and the ties on them down and over the chair's leg. They were tapered, so it got easier as it went down.

With that done, she rolled over, quickly pulled her hands over her feet and could stand up with her hands tied in front now. Her sister's eyes widened, and she stared at her in shock. Rosalina shrugged. "Not sure it helps much," she said, "because I'm still tied up." Rosalina hopped over and untied the gag on her sister's mouth. "Don't suppose you have anything sharp enough to cut these, do you?" And she pointed at the ties on her feet.

"No," Melinda gasped.

When Rosalina studied her tied feet further, she realized, without the chair leg involved, the ties had loosened just enough so that she could shift one of the loops of the zip ties, and, just like that, one foot at a time, she was free. With her feet free, she went to work on her hands, trying a similar method. It wasn't as easy, but she walked around, checked on her sister, and could untie her because she was tied with ropes. With that done, they got Melinda's legs free. Still Rosalina's hands weren't free, but her sister was completely free.

"Oh, my God," Melinda said. "Where did you learn to do that?"

Rosalina stopped, looked back at the chair, and shrugged. "You know how I always loved puzzles."

"Those are hardly puzzles," she snapped.

"No," Rosalina said, "but, in this case, their solution was exactly what we needed." She went back to chewing the heavy plastic on her wrists. It didn't take long before it snapped. With their hands and feet free, she looked at the door. "So, what next?"

Immediately Melinda raced to the door. "We have to get out of here."

"Oh, I agree," she said. She picked up a chair and studying it for a moment, untwisted one of the legs until it came off.

Her sister looked at her. "What are you doing?"

"We need weapons," she said. Handing the first chair leg to her sister, she then unscrewed two more. "Now let's go," she said, and her sister reached for the door.

CHAPTER 2

THE MOMENT THE unlocked door opened, Rosalina expected to face a guard or to be charged by somebody racing toward them. But, as they peered around the door, they saw nothing but a nasty dark-gray hallway, as if they were in the basement of some large building. Several ducts and HVAC system components lined the ceiling above them. She also saw several more doors. They slipped out, and she walked to the door beside them and opened it, only to find it was an empty room. They quickly checked all the other doors down this hallway, looking for their parents, but found no sign of anyone.

Each sister armed only with what they had, a chair leg and two, they headed toward the Exit sign.

"This looks like a big hotel," Melinda said.

"It might be," Rosalina said. "I don't really care. I just want to get out of here."

"You want out of here?" Melinda said. "My children and fiancé are back at the hotel."

"For all we know," Rosalina said, "we could be in the same damn hotel."

They pushed on the Exit door, surprised that it allowed them to get out. One of those lever-operating systems, where you push it in, and the door unlocked and let them out. They raced up the stairs. On every floor they kept looking for another way out.

The next level was obviously a much lighter atmosphere. "It looks like we were three floors down from ground level," Rosalina said. She headed out into an underground parking lot. Quickly they slipped through and were in the area where the vehicles were parked. Immediately they hid between two vehicles.

"How is it that we got out so fast?" her sister asked.

"I suspect they wanted Dad and Mom instead," she said, "but, because we were all together, they took us all."

Melinda stared at her in shock.

"The good news," Rosalina said, "is that we can get you back to Steve and the kids."

"We need a phone," she said. "How do we know we're even safe here?"

"We're not," Rosalina said. "Come on. Let's go this way." She led them around the vehicles and up to the car park exit, where nobody was in the little booth at the side. It was all automated. She ducked under the gate, and, just like that, they were out on the busy street. Looking around, she said, "Well, it looks like we might still be in Honolulu."

"How can you tell?" Melinda asked, gasping beside her.

"I can't really," she said, "but it's one very busy town center at least." She turned to look around and saw a couple businessmen walking toward her. She stepped out smartly in front of them and said, "Excuse me, we have an emergency. Could we possibly borrow your phone?"

One of the men immediately handed his to her. "What kind of emergency?" he asked, looking puzzled.

She pointed at her sister. "We were kidnapped." But she was already dialing. She tried the police emergency number first. But it was busy. "We need to get through to 9-1-1," she said.

"Maybe," her sister said, "but let me try Steve." She immediately dialed Steve. As soon as his voice came on, she cried out, "Steve! I'm here!" She looked at the businessman. "Do you know what corner or what street we're on?" They quickly gave her the street location.

Rosalina looked at him. "I hate to ask, but are we still in Honolulu?"

Bemused, both men nodded.

Once Melinda made arrangements with Steve for a pickup, she returned the phone to the men.

When she didn't stop to thank them, Rosalina added, "Thank you. Really. Thank you, so much."

The men just shrugged and said, "Sorry this happened to you," they said. "Is there anything else we can do?"

"I'd like to make one more phone call, if you don't mind," Rosalina said. "Our parents were kidnapped with us, and I'm wondering where they are."

He handed her the phone immediately. She dialed her father's number, and it rang and rang, then went to voicemail. "Dad—" she said, and then she stopped. She hit End, terminating the call. "I don't want to let the kidnappers know we're free," she said, looking back at her sister. Her sister had her arms wrapped around her slim frame and nodded. "Not until we're safe," Rosalina said. "You know they'll come after us."

One of the men spoke. "Maybe. Can you identify the kidnappers?"

Both women shook their heads. "We were taken off the street while walking home from dinner," Rosalina said. "We didn't see much." The two men stayed with them until a black SUV careened around the corner.

Before it even stopped completely, Steve jumped out and raced toward Melinda, picking her up and holding her tight. She was crying and talking and threw her arms around his neck.

The two businessmen just watched.

Another man hopped out the back of the SUV and joined them, his gaze direct and with a clear sense of purpose. He reached out a hand. "I'm Gavin," he said. "I'm here to recover your parents."

"I hope you mean that in the best of ways," Rosalina said, staring at him. She gripped his hand. "Neither of them are in the best of health."

"How did you get free?"

She frowned, then looked back at the underground parking garage. "I might be able to lead you back to the same room," she said, "but I'm not going in there alone without some law enforcement. I don't want to get picked up again," she said. "We were down below, three floors, I think. They left us in a little cement room. We were tied to our chairs."

At that, her sister broke in. "I don't know how she did it," Melinda said. "She was amazing. One minute we were sitting there, all tied up. The next thing I knew, she stood and did this flip, and, all of a sudden, she was free. And then she got me free. We checked all the basement rooms on our floor, looking for our parents, and then we found the parking garage by going up a few flights."

A second man joined Gavin. He smiled at them, nodded, and said, "I'm Shane. Why don't you lead us back down to where you were."

Rosalina looked at her sister. "You go with Steve back to the hotel and make sure the kids are okay," she said. "I'll take these men down again." Her sister hesitated, but Rosalina smiled and encouraged her to go. Then she turned to the first man. "Are you sure you don't want to bring a few cops with us?" she asked. "I really don't want to get taken again."

"We won't be needing cops," Gavin said, his voice flat.

She studied him carefully, then nodded. "If you say so. Don't let me down." She turned, and, without another word to her sister, she headed back down.

GAVIN EXCHANGED A look with Shane, the two of them a little unsure about this very direct person. But they followed her quickly. She motioned to the door that they had come out of into the parking garage. It was locked. She frowned.

Gavin said, "It's normal to have some of these doors be locked all the time, but, if you're on the inside, you can get out." He quickly unlocked it, without letting her see how.

With the door open, she said, "Now three flights of stairs down." She immediately took the lead and headed down the stairs.

Gavin raised an eyebrow and followed her. He checked the surrounding areas, but there was absolutely nothing different about this. It was simply an empty stairwell in a very large hotel with commercial buildings on the street level and shipping, parking, and storage units down below. Gavin wasn't even sure what all three underground floors were used for, but it wasn't uncommon in large cities to have a setup like this for laundry purposes, for additional storage, for garbage collection, for deliveries.

As soon as they hit the floor that she wanted, she opened the hallway door and stepped through. He followed with Shane right behind him. She looked left and right, then frowned and turned to the right and walked over a few doorways. At the third door she stopped. "This one."

He used his sleeve to open up the doorway and to step inside. Sure enough, he saw cut ties and a chair missing three legs. He looked at the one remaining leg, frowning.

She shrugged and said, "I took three with us, just in case. Two for me and one for my sister. I ditched them in the parking garage."

"Interesting." He walked the small room, nodded, and said, "We'll get forensics in here, just in case," he said. "I suspect nothing viable is left, but you never know."

"Good enough." She followed the men back to the hallway. Outside, Shane marked the door in a subtle way that wouldn't be obvious, but they could direct the cops to it.

Gavin urged her to walk with him and asked, "Do you have any other recollection of this building?"

She shook her head. "What I don't know is whether I was left so that I could get out," she said, "or if they were planning to come back, assuming we couldn't get out?"

"We'll leave somebody here to watch," Gavin said, opening the stairwell door for her. "But how did you get out?"

She shrugged and explained, but she appreciated the quick gleam of approval in his eyes. She gave him a lopsided look. "Another thing I don't understand is why Melinda was gagged and I wasn't."

"Did it help you at all either way? Did it change anything?"

She shook her head. "No," she said. "I didn't need a gag one way or the other."

He nodded and tucked away that bit of information as they took another flight of stairs and neared the ground floor. "Did you see your kidnappers at all?"

"Not really. Only that they wore all black with hoods, and I only saw that much for a quick second before they adjusted my blindfold," she said. "I might identify the van though."

"We've already got it," he said, pushing open the Exit door to enter the parking area. "They traded it for another vehicle. What about that one?"

She shook her head. "I didn't know they did that. I was fighting them, and one of the men smacked me hard against the head," she said. "I hit the side of the van and must have blacked out. When I woke up, I was in that room down there."

"Okay," he said. "Let's get you back to the hotel and get you a medical check. Then we'll have a bunch more questions for you."

"Anything I can do to help," she replied, now staring out at the street.

"Any idea why someone would take your parents?"

"No," she said. "I'd still like to go back and check every other floor."

"We've already got two local teams coming in," he said quietly. "We'll find your parents, if they're in that building." He watched as that sank in. "The real question is, who could be behind this?" he asked. "Are you sure you have no idea?"

"No, I've been trying to figure it out this whole time."

"Problems with the company?"

"No. Nothing I know of."

"That's a really good point," Shane said. "How much do you have to do with the business part of the company?"

"I work there," she said, "but honestly I don't deal with the board at all."

"By choice?" he asked.

She shot him a look. "I can't do politics," she said. "I'm a very direct person, and I don't play games."

"Well, we appreciate that," Gavin said. "And we do find that often these kinds of scenarios are really power plays."

"Which just sucks," she said, "because it puts me out of my depth. I don't have a clue how to handle people like that."

"What about your father? Does he play those games?"

She shrugged. "I guess it's possible," she said, "but it's not necessarily a normal state for him. He likes the game—I mean, like the art of negotiating—but, more than that, he is dedicated to the type of research we do."

Gavin continued, "Do you think anybody is after your research?"

She frowned at that and stared at him, considering his question.

Her eyes were the palest of blue. How had he not noticed before? They were almost a soft gray.

"Anything is possible," she said, "but you have to understand that we have any number of research projects in progress at any given time."

"Any hostile takeovers?" Shane asked.

She switched her gaze to him. "Not that I know of. But, again, I don't have anything to do with the board."

"Would your father tell you," Gavin asked, "if a takeover play were going on?"

She shrugged. "I'm not sure," she said. "I would like to think so."

"And what about espionage?"

She wrinkled up her face at that. "Another nasty element of humanity I don't like," she said. "But we did have a problem a couple years ago. I don't know all the details, but one of the scientists was selling some of our work to a competing company."

"That competing company," Shane said, "do you think they would be involved in something like this?"

"They went broke about six months ago," she said.

"So a dissatisfied scientist who wanted to advance?" Gavin asked. "Or a plant from outside perhaps? Is there a noncompete section in your employment contracts when you hire someone?"

She stared at him. "I guess you'll have to run through the personnel files and talk to the admin staff," she said. "I have no clue. Again, dealing with people isn't my thing."

"Got it," he said. "That doesn't necessarily let you off the hook though."

"In what way?"

"I've got more questions," Gavin said with a smile. "Did you know any of the people who worked for that other company? Were any of them trying to get on with your company? Did you have to fire anybody recently at your family's company?"

She stared at him for a long moment. "I don't think you understand," she said. "I have a large lab, where two people work with me. They have worked with me for over a decade. We all finished school together. I trust them, and, as far as I know, they have no ambitions beyond the type of work we are doing. We are very dedicated to the research."

"Well, we'll need names and contact information," he said.

She shrugged. "That's not hard. Get everything from my assistant."

"And is the assistant one of those two people?"

She shook her head. "No. I do tend to go through a few

of those," she admitted.

"Why?" Gavin asked bluntly.

"Because they don't like doing their work," she said just as bluntly. "I don't have any tolerance for lazy ineffectual people with a million excuses for why the work didn't get done."

"Interesting," he said, though inside he agreed. He felt the same way about a lot of the world. "And your current assistant," he said, "how long has she worked for you?"

"Two years thankfully," she said. "The last one was about six months, and the one before that about three months."

"So you're happy with this one?"

"So far, yes," she said. "I just don't know when that'll change."

"Are you expecting it to change?" Gavin asked, with a quizzical expression.

"She's got a new boyfriend," she said, "so chances are it will change. One of the things I will not tolerate is personal interactions during the day. If you're working for me, you're not on a chat forum, and you're not on a social media site, and you sure as hell had better not be texting all day long."

"Right," he said with a smile. "Got it."

CHAPTER 3

ROSALINA KNEW THE line of questioning was necessary, but surely he had something else, another avenue to look at. "My parents could have been taken for any number of reasons," she said suddenly. She had both Gavin's and Shane's attention with that. They were waiting in the parking garage at the moment. She knew teams were already coming to look at the forensics, the cameras, and all the rest of that stuff. It was amazing how much tourist foot traffic was here, with people coming and going from the hotel and taking their own transportation.

Waiting until they were alone for the moment, she lowered her voice. "I don't like Melinda's husband," she said.

"Steve?" Gavin asked. "Steve Arbrey?"

She shook her head. "No. Steve is fine. Great even. I didn't like Barry. Her legal husband. Of course they're divorced by now," she said with a wave of her hand. "I forget how fast time flies."

"And why didn't you like him?"

"He was arrogant and had nothing good to say about women in the workforce. Personally I think he is a racist and a sexist, not to mention a misogynist."

Gavin smiled. "All those together?"

"They tend to go together," she said seriously. Because, in her experience, they did.

"All right, but you must have another reason beyond that to think he'd do something as extreme as this."

"My parents made it very clear, when Melinda and Barry divorced, that my parents would support their daughter and grandchildren in whatever way necessary, but that Barry wouldn't get a penny. Not from Melinda or the company."

"Did he have any money of his own?"

She shook her head. "Not that I know of."

"So they lived off her money?"

"She has our grandparents' home," Rosalina said. "It's worth quite a bit. He worked, but he didn't make nearly the money she did."

"Any dissent between them?"

"Lots," she said. "They fought all the time. When it became obvious that it was time for them to part, he wanted the kids, and she wouldn't let him have them. My parents went to bat for her with expensive lawyers, and Barry ended up out in the cold with nothing."

The two men gave her a flat stare.

She shrugged. "What can I say? That is my parents for you."

"That gives us insights into their characters in a big way."

"But you have to round that out with the human factor that their grandchildren's health, happiness, and welfare were at stake," she said.

"Reason for the divorce?"

"Just a marriage breakdown, as far as I know," she said. "I don't think he was ever violent or anything like that."

"So, just that it was time to be apart because they were better alone than they were together?"

"I believe so. Though I think jealousy was getting to be a

big issue."

"In what way?"

"Melinda was moving on with her life and moving up in the company. But, of course, it's her parents' company," she said, trying to distance herself from the scenario so she could get a more detached view. "So, yes, obviously it's my company too, my parents' company as well," she said. "But, from an onlooker's viewpoint, it looked like Melinda had the golden pathway provided for her, and she could do no wrong and didn't have to earn it."

"And was it like that for her?"

Rosalina hesitated. "Yes, in a way," she admitted. "Two sisters, one large company. Both of us in the field."

"But she wasn't originally?"

"No. My dad was a researcher. A mechanical engineer with a science background. When she was born missing her lower leg, he got into this prosthetics field in a big way. So, although she's not technically a scientist in the same way as I am, she does a certain amount of research," she said half-heartedly, clearly not wanting to get into a detailed explanation of it all. "Melinda was the impetus for the company. There would be no company but for her. However, she handles a lot of the marketing more than she does the science, that's all."

The two men continued to stare at her, as if waiting. She gave them a flat stare back. They could ask questions if they wanted to learn more, but she'd be damned if she'd voluntarily get into her family dynamics.

"Any problems between the two of you?" Gavin asked expectantly.

"What problems?" she asked. But her heart sank as she saw the knowing look on Gavin's face.

"Come on. Fess up," he said. "We'll need all the dirt."

"Fine," she said. "Melinda went into the science part of the business and didn't do very well. She barely scraped through school, and, on the job, she made a couple very significant mistakes that cost the company big. At that point in time my father moved her to marketing, where she couldn't cause any damage in the lab."

"So then, the younger sister comes along, completely brilliant where science is concerned, stepping into the role that Melinda had sought for herself. And, in no time, you are in charge of R&D."

"How did you know I run the R&D department?" she asked, frowning at him. "Dad had a very logical reason for moving me into that position."

"Logical, yes, but potentially harmful in terms of the relationship between the two of you sisters," Gavin said.

"Melinda was married with a family," she said, "and research and development wasn't her thing. She still wanted to be part of the company, but it was obvious she couldn't do that job. What was I supposed to do?"

"Did you rat her out?" Shane asked.

At that, she could feel her eyes widen in shock. "Of course not," she said. "I didn't have to anyway. Her gaffe cost the company a small fortune in the lab, and a lot of expensive materials were damaged. It is what it is. I didn't create the problem. She did. She wasn't in the right job, and honestly she is much better suited for the position she holds now."

"And, of course," Shane continued, "it leaves you free and clear to take over the R&D department as the wonder child."

At that, she narrowed her gaze at him. "Really? What is

it with you two? I don't think I like what you're implying."

"Maybe not," Shane said quietly. "But it could and does appear to some that you deliberately had your older sister removed from the lab, then stepped into her place. Now everybody turns to you for the latest and greatest news on the R&D side."

"People can say whatever the hell they want," she said briskly. "They will anyway. But I've never done anything to intentionally hurt my sister. More than ten years are between us, so we might as well be from two separate families. By the time I was old enough to understand I had a sister, she was never around and always off for various activities," she said, with a wave of her hand. "If it wasn't ballet with a prosthetic, it was swimming lessons or riding horses," she said. "She was never home. Plus, she was very close to our parents, who treated her as really special, I guess because of her disability. And me? I was just the baby who was in the way all the time."

"And did that bother you?" Gavin asked.

"No, of course not," she said. "Everybody was compensating because of her disability. That's what people do. It's to be expected."

"So, not wanting to appear like your sister, you hid your smarts, I imagine."

She turned her gaze on Gavin. "And who are you to assume that I have any?" He gave her a small smile. She shrugged. "So school was easy for me."

"Were you ever tested?" Gavin asked, with a smile.

She raised an eyebrow. "You mean, like Mensa? No," she said. "Why would I want to be labeled or restricted by a number?"

Gavin laughed at that. "I have no problems with you

being super intelligent," he announced. "I'm quite comfortable being me and doing what I do," he said, "but I'm guessing some people feel threatened by your obvious brainpower."

"I hope not," she said, frowning. "I try hard not to appear too super intelligent. It does not make you friends."

"No," he said gently. "But I don't think you suffer fools gladly. And I imagine there's an edge to your voice when things don't go the way you expect them to go."

"If it's in my research lab, and it doesn't go in the direction I expect, I simply want to know why," she said. "But, if it happens to be situations where people haven't done what they were supposed to do, that is a different story."

"And then they hear the edge in your tone. Is that the idea?" Shane asked.

"I'm not bitchy, if that's what you're asking," she said. "That's why I work with the people I work with. They know my expectations, and they do what they are supposed to do. I certainly show appreciation when something works out or when my expectations are exceeded, and I try not to gouge into them if they've done something stupid and made an honest mistake. Because the people I work with," she stated firmly, "are professionals. What I can't stand are insipid half-assed people, claiming to have skills that they don't have, so, when they get on a job, they mess things up more than anything."

At that, Gavin gave a long-drawn-out breath. "So, your sister, I guess." Rosalina glared at him but could feel some heat climbing up her neck. He nodded. "You don't have to say anything else. I get it."

"But do you?" she asked. "Do you know what it's like to be in a department where your sister is the one screwing up things? And she won't leave, even though she knows it's the wrong place for her, all because she doesn't want her parents to know she can't handle it?"

"Meaning, they just continued to let her do her job badly without recriminations?"

"She figured they only gave her the job because of her disability in the first place. That really bothered her, so she wanted to do a good job and to prove that she could do it."

"I would imagine that nobody wants a handout all the time," he said.

"She loves handouts," she said. "And I have no problem with her getting the handouts. But I want her well away from my department."

At that, Gavin laughed out loud.

"That surprises you?"

"No, not at all," he said. "I'm sure a lot of people in the world would agree with you. And I'm not one who suffers fools gracefully either." He shoved his hands in his pockets, as he studied the area around them. "I want to get you back to the hotel," he said. "Is there any chance that you've recognized any of the kidnappers' faces? Anything we could use a sketch artist for?"

"No," she said. "I told you that I could probably have identified the van, but that's it."

"Anything inside the van of interest?" Shane asked suddenly. "Was it just the four of you? Were there any packages, any kind of bags or name tags?"

She looked at him in surprise. "Rope," she said. "Lots of rope."

He frowned at that. "What kind?"

"That slippery yellow poly stuff that I hate," she said. "You know? You tie a knot, and then it comes untied because the surface is so slick?"

"Was it loose, one big roll, a drum, or a bunch of bundles tied up?"

"Bundles tied up," she said instantly. "And duct tape. I wonder what that was for."

"Maybe for you and for your parents," Gavin suggested.

"But a cloth bandanna was used for Melinda's gag. I hope they don't use duct tape on my parents," she said. "My dad has a mustache and a beard. That'll hurt like hell to get it off."

Even Gavin winced at that. "Absolutely," he said. "But, on the other hand, hopefully if they're taking it off, it means they're safe somewhere."

"Or the kidnappers just want to ask them questions."

"Okay. Back to the ex-husband," Gavin said. "Did he have a problem with his wife's personality?"

"No," she said. "Why would anybody have a problem with Melinda's personality? She's all about emotions."

Shane laughed out loud at that. "And what are you?"

"I'm all soul," she said, "but I keep it hidden." Then she stopped, surprised. "Wow, I didn't expect to say that."

"An interesting statement," Gavin said, studying her intently.

She wished he would stop doing that. Just something about his eyes was getting her. "Why is that?" she asked.

"Because a heart full of love and trust and patience is not necessarily the same thing as a soul full of principles and the core of what a person is."

"Well, for me, soul is the purpose, the deeper purpose of why you do things in life," she said. "The checks and balances, the karma that'll meet you at the end of the golden gates."

When she realized the two men were looking at her with confusion on their faces, she explained. "I tend to think of the heart as being shared in individual relationships—like with a spouse, a child, a parent—but your soul is you interacting with humanity, like your larger purpose for being here on the planet in action," she said.

"Interesting," Gavin murmured.

Rosalina wasn't sure if the men liked her explanation or not, but it was the way she felt. She was doing something on a much larger scale.

Shane shook his head and looked around. "Come on. Here's our ride." And, sure enough, the black SUV from before pulled up. It had the same license plate, but, as the doors opened, a different driver exited. Gavin headed straight toward him and demanded, "ID."

The driver stared at him for a long moment. "Seriously?"

"Absolutely," Gavin said. "ID now."

He groaned but pulled out his badge for Gavin to see.

"So, just out of curiosity," Shane said to Rosalina, "I understand you were married before?"

"Yes," she said coolly. "And I can see that your next question will be about heart, and the answer is no. I thought it was a good idea, and I thought we could make it work. But, no, we didn't."

After that, there wasn't a whole lot anybody could say. They were inside the vehicle, once the driver's ID had been well and truly checked.

AS THE BLACK SUV arrived at the hotel, Gavin hopped out first, then escorted her inside, going straight to the elevator and up. She looked at him. "Is there a reason you're not allowing me to talk to people or to see anyone?"

"Is there a reason you haven't asked to contact anyone?"

"But I did," she said.

"No, that was your sister contacting Steve," he said, looking at her.

She shrugged. "Where did Shane go?"

He liked the fact that she had changed the subject. "He's checking out security."

"Oh," she said. "Am I in danger?"

"Quite possibly, yes," he said. "So, what's the problem between you and your parents?"

"I'm not missing a limb," she said bluntly.

He sucked in his breath and stared at her. "Seriously?"

"When you're the very self-sufficient child and obviously intelligent, in many families that would make you the golden child. But, in a family where the other sibling is both firstborn and disabled, the first sibling got all the love and attention."

"So why did your mother even get pregnant again?"

"She didn't want to," she said. "Apparently some mishap occurred with her contraception."

"So, you were labeled an *accident*?" he asked, wonder and anger in his gaze.

"That's a good word for it, yes," she said. She laughed. "And people look at me with pity, as if to say, 'Oh, you poor child,' or something."

"Well, I don't have any intention of doing that," he said. "You obviously don't need it, wouldn't appreciate it, and I highly doubt it even applies under the circumstances."

At that, she laughed. "That's very true," she said. "I learned to become self-sufficient very early on. But nannies will do that too."

He waited for her to say more, but, when she didn't, he said, "You were raised by nannies?"

"Yep. My parents were already working in the labs all the time."

"With your sister?"

"Yep," she said. "My sister was either there with them or off doing stuff."

"I hear your words, but I don't hear the emotions behind them," he said.

"Because emotions don't help anything," she said, and she stepped out of the elevator first before he could. He immediately grabbed her arm and kept her at his side while he checked around. "It'll be fine," she said. "If anybody's waiting for us, they'll probably be in my room." And she marched toward her room, then stopped abruptly. "Why would we return to my room, where the kidnappers can find me easily? Doesn't seem wise. Or safe."

Gavin chuckled. "You've got me and Shane now." She frowned but seemed to accept that. "Don't suppose you still have a key, do you?"

She shook her head. "Aren't you one of those Secret Service guys? Can't you just get me in there?"

Instead, he opened her room with a keycard.

She looked at it, frowning. "You better not have the second card to my room."

"Why is that?"

"Because nobody gets a key to my room but me," she said smartly and went to shut the door.

But his foot was in the way, and he pushed it open. "You aren't going in alone, so I don't want to hear any talk about that."

She just glared at him.

He studied her, wondering why she seemed so uncaring. Then, just as he caught the ever-so-slight tremor of her lips, he realized with shock that she was not uncaring, cold, or disconnected from everything. No. Her lack of emotional displays wasn't about her caring too little but how she cared too much.

With a small groan, he tugged her into his arms. She tried to fight back and then just gave up the ghost and bawled. He held her against his heart, wondering at a child who had been alone so much of her life that she'd learned to protect herself and to give this outward appearance of having absolutely no feelings. When, in fact, the opposite was true, and inside she was still the little girl just bawling her eyes out because she wasn't as well loved as her sister.

When she was finally drained, she stepped back, turning her face away, mumbling, "I'm sorry. I don't know what just happened."

"You had a perfectly human reaction to the stress of being kidnapped," he said patiently. He walked through the small room. "You didn't get a big fancy suite like the rest of your family?"

"No," she said, sagging onto the side of the bed. "I prefer to spend money in the lab rather than on extras, like a huge room I don't need."

"Understood," he said. "And I presume the company isn't paying for it?"

"The company is paying for it," she said, "but it's coming from departmental funds. Like I said, departmental funds need to be directed into the research."

He loved that about her. Too often people thought that travel expense money was for the spending and that they should get their fair share of it. In her case, she just wanted it for her research. "So, what kind of research are you working on?"

She shrugged and didn't say anything.

"I'm sure you have a little more soul behind it than that."

She laughed. "Now you're turning my words around on me, aren't you?"

"Not necessarily," he said. "I just wondered what kind of research you were doing."

"But you already know it's got to do with prosthetics," she said. "So what else is the issue?"

"No issue," he said. "I have a lot of war buddies, like navy and other branches of the military, all who could use your services."

"And that's partly why I do what I do," she said.

"That is one of the things I wanted to ask you," he said. "What started you on this pathway? I highly doubt it was because of your sister."

She shot him a shuttered look. "That doesn't sound very nice."

He smiled, shook his head, and said, "I'm not putting any criticism or judgment on it," he said. "But I suspect you have some reason to be the way you are, particularly after all these years."

"My husband ran over a little boy and crushed his leg."

"No, before that," he said.

She frowned up at him. "Well, he really did."

"Maybe," Gavin said, "but you were driven years and years before that, so it has nothing to do with something that happened in the last five years. No way."

She crossed her arms over her chest in a protective stance

and glared at him. "Why are you digging into me?" she snapped. "What does that have to do with finding the kidnappers?"

"I have to know everything about everybody in order to know what's important," he explained quietly.

She shook her head. "Just sounds like you're being nosy to me."

He grinned. "I like you," he said. "So I want to know everything there is to know about you."

At that, her arms tightened under her chest, and she glared at him.

"So it's that important?" he asked.

"What do you mean?"

"It's one of those little secrets you hold close to your heart," he said, "and you haven't shared it with anybody." He moved around the room, quietly observing. "Maybe your ex's accident gives you something to tell people, and I'm sure that has a lot to do with it," he said, "but I doubt it's the real reason, the initial foundational reason."

She shrugged and sank back on the bed. "It's not a secret at all. It's just not necessarily wanting to share every detail when I don't know you that well."

And, with that, he realized she really wouldn't give it up. "Okay. But, before this is over," he said, "you'll tell me because we're going to get to know each other real well."

"Don't hold your breath," she said, staring up at the ceiling. "Look. I need a shower," she said after a few minutes.

"Feel free," he said. Getting up, he walked into the bathroom, where he checked that all was okay. "You know I'm not leaving you here alone," he said. "So, whenever you're ready to have your shower, go ahead."

She looked at him in surprise. "You'll be here when I

come out?"

"I most definitely will," he said. And, for a split second, he caught that ever-so-slight glimpse of relief in her eyes as he nodded. "I promise."

She got up and walked to the dresser, and, from where he stood, he could see the neatly folded clothes. She collected a set of clothing and walked into the bathroom. She never said a word and just closed the door tightly behind her.

"Don't lock it please," he said.

The door popped open, and she stared at him. "Why not?"

And he could see she really didn't understand. "Because, if I have to get to you for any reason," he said, "I won't have time for niceties."

She chewed on her bottom lip and then closed the door quietly behind her.

He pulled out his phone, wishing he had his laptop with him. He sent Shane a message, updating him on where he was and what Rosalina was doing. Shane responded to say he would be there in five. Gavin walked over to the bathroom and spoke.

"Don't panic if you hear the door. Shane's on his way and will be here at any moment."

"Okay," she called out. "Why don't you order coffee then?" she said. "I'll need some food and sustenance."

"Done," he said. When the knock came at the door, he opened it to let Shane in. "I was just ordering some coffee," Gavin said.

Shane looked around the room and nodded. "Not the same as what her parents and her sister have."

"No. Apparently the funds for their traveling trips comes from their respective departmental budgets," he said. "She wanted all her funding to go to research, so she limits the frills and keeps expenses within reason."

He nodded approvingly. "Glad to hear that," he said, "because you know what people tend to do when it comes to all that travel money sitting there."

"I know," he said. "Anything new?"

"All the cameras from the basement location where she and her sister were kept are down," Shane said. "Individual cameras themselves were damaged, rather than the software."

"So somebody on the spot, not somebody in the control center?" Gavin observed.

"No hackers," Shane confirmed. "We have the family on camera here, leaving the hotel for dinner. No sign of them being followed. We did contact the restaurant where they ate dinner and have video feed from there as they left. They went out the front door, and the security cameras cover the first twenty feet."

"But nothing past that, right?" Gavin confirmed.

"No, nothing past that. Nothing on the traffic cameras along the way either. No sign of them until we get close to the hotel again, where they were picked up and tossed into the vehicle. And we already know what happened then."

"So, we still have no idea why they were taken or why the girls were left in that one room."

"No," Shane replied.

"I do find it interesting that Rosalina wasn't gagged," Gavin continued, "and that she's the one who got out of her bindings. Whereas, the other sister was gagged and did not get free without her younger sister's help."

"Yes, but why?"

"Maybe Melinda went off on them," Gavin suggested. "And they decided to shut her up with a gag."

"And yet we haven't had much time with Melinda," Shane said. "But which one of the sisters would you want to shut up most if you were the bad guy?"

Gavin nodded toward the shower. "Her."

"Exactly." Shane said, "Interesting, isn't it?"

"Do you think they wanted to see if she could get out?" Gavin asked.

Shane nodded with a one-arm shrug.

"It occurred to me too," Gavin said. "But I don't know why anybody would care. Any number of people could have gotten out of those bindings."

"Right, unless somebody wanted to see her or her sister suffer. Are we back to the ex-husbands again?"

"Ah, maybe," Gavin said, pulling out his phone and texting. "I'll ask Lennox to have someone look into it now."

"Good," Shane said. "But we'll also have to figure out where the parents are, and they seem to have disappeared off the face of the earth."

"Well, they'll be somewhere," Gavin replied. "What I don't want us to find is that the bodies have been dumped somewhere before we've gotten anywhere on this."

"Exactly," he said.

"But we have absolutely no sign of the parents in the building where the girls were held. None of the other rooms showed any sign of them being there. Forensics is still on it, of course, but running through a million fingerprints and bits and pieces of DNA will take forever."

"Well, we need to put a rush on it," Shane said.

"Yeah. Any other updates?"

"I've already started investigations into the other members of the board," Shane said. "I contacted the chairman and the CFO, and neither knew anything. Of course both are now in damage-control mode, in case their stocks take a hit and all."

"Has it been on the news yet?"

"Not yet," Shane said, "but you know it won't be long. The media will be all over this."

"What is the general tone on this group right now?"

"Generally the company is fairly well-liked, and we're not hearing many negative reviews. They do a certain amount of charity work, and that always goes down well with the public. A lot of their clients are military and kids too."

"Any dissenters?" Gavin paced around the room. "Anybody got something bad to say? Anybody claiming they were fired unfairly or anything like that?"

"I've hooked Lennox on to the HR department to talk about any threatening letters or unhappy employees. He'll get back with me if he finds any red flags," Shane said. "But I'm not seeing any old or new beefs popping up on the internet."

"But no company is lily-white," Gavin said. "Somebody out there has a motive for doing this. Either it's personal or it'll be business."

"Unless they're involved in something nonprofit," Shane said, pondering.

"And that damn well better be on the list of things handed over by the background checks on the family. What were their activities? What clubs did they belong to?"

"Sure, we'll cast a wide net," Shane said. "But, if we don't have any way to cull it down as we sort through it all, I don't know how we'll find anything relevant."

"True," he said. "Other suggestions?"

"Don't have any."

"I was expecting a ransom demand or a blackmail attempt of some kind," Gavin said, thinking about it. "Feels like we're missing a big chunk of their lives."

"Maybe. Hopefully Lennox will get us the information on the exes soon. Particularly the one unhappy about the disposition of his children. He looks like a good avenue."

"Possibly," Gavin said. "When you consider the fact that he's not only lost his kids but, when his in-laws made it so clear about what they would do, I mean, that's basically putting a target on the in-laws' backs."

"Yeah," he said. "But that divorce was like six, seven years ago, right? We're missing something more current."

"We're focused on the daughters, but they were the ones released. Or, at the very least, not held competently. So, were they just in the wrong place at the wrong time? Or is there something else?"

Shane tilted his head. "Good questions. I have no answers."

Gavin still had a nagging suspicion that something specifically dealt with why the one sister wasn't gagged and the other was. "We need to talk to the other sister," he said.

"I just came from there," Shane said. "That Steve guy, the fiancé, is very particular about nobody bothering her right now."

Gavin stared at him. "For real?"

Shane nodded. "Yeah, he wants her to lie down first."

Gavin hopped to his feet. "You stay here," he said. "I don't want Rosalina left alone. Order coffee and maybe some food. I'll go talk to the sister."

"But—" Shane said, but Gavin was already at the door.

He turned back and said, "No buts. That's bullshit, and Steve knows better. I'm not standing for it." He headed out, slamming the door behind him.

CHAPTER 4

ROSALINA HEARD THE hotel door slam and quickly dressed. She opened the bathroom door to see Shane, sitting there, using his laptop. "Hey, a laptop," she said. "Did you bring that?"

He nodded. "We have a lot of work to do." He glanced at her and smiled. "Coffee and food are coming soon."

"Perfect," she said, still running a comb through her long hair. She usually kept it in a severe bun or plaited behind her head. It often got in the way at work if she didn't, but, when it was loose and freshly washed like this, she loved to have it free. Walking over, she sat down at the small table. "Was that Gavin slamming the door?"

Shane chuckled. "Yes."

"Why is he upset?"

"Your sister's fiancé wouldn't let me talk to her."

"What? Steve wouldn't let you talk to Melinda?"

He nodded. "Said he would bring in the police department to stop me from disturbing her because she needed her rest."

She stared at him, shaking her head. "That is classic Melinda all over again."

"Well, Melinda may have just met her match," Shane said, with a nod toward the door. "Gavin's got absolutely no truck with that kind of crap."

"I could go there too," she said, jumping to her feet. "She'll talk to me."

"I'm sure," he said, "but Gavin wants to talk to her."

"Meaning talk to her, not me," she said, studying his face.

He nodded. "Not because he doesn't want to hear what you have to say," he said, "but he wants to hear what she has to say without you around."

Her shoulders drew in. "She'll have plenty to say." She thought about all the years she had tried to be a good sister and had apparently failed because Melinda really didn't have any tolerance or patience for Rosalina.

"Maybe," Shane said, his tone gentle. "But that doesn't mean that Gavin will be swayed by it."

"She'll say the same thing everybody would say," she said, with a wave of her hand. "I'm a cold bitch."

"Do people actually say that to you?"

"Not to my face," she said, with a quiet smile. "But behind my back? Yes."

"I'm sorry," he said. "That's just not fair."

"I never thought it was either, but people get to be people," she said, "and you hear things." Her voice dropped off as she thought about the number of times she'd overheard people talking, 'You know? The whole water-cooler thing."

"I'm sorry," he said.

"It doesn't matter," she said, with a dismissive smile.

"It does matter," Shane replied. "People don't have to be assholes."

She laughed at that. "Maybe they don't have to be," she said, "but I think sometimes they prefer it that way. Just something about our current state of affairs lets people think that they can say and do anything, whether it's the truth or lies, and that nobody will get hurt by it. And, if someone is hurt, it's too damn bad."

"I hear you," he said. "The fact of the matter is, obviously some hard feelings exist between you and your sister."

"I don't think so," she said, setting him straight. "I think I'm just a nuisance to my sister. An upstart. Meanwhile, she was always the older sister I could never quite connect to. So she was the golden child, and I was just less somehow."

"And yet, with your brainpower, you would think your father would be proud of you and your accomplishments."

She chuckled. "He is, of course, but it's also what he expects from me. You see? When you're handicapped or disabled in our family, nobody expects much from you. So, when you do really well, or even are mediocre, you're to be praised high and above because, of course, you were dealing with so much more difficulty in getting a job accomplished."

He chuckled. "She's got them all wrapped around her little finger, doesn't she?"

She looked at him in surprise. "You figured that out, huh?"

"Yeah. Especially Steve."

"Gavin won't hurt Steve, will he?" she asked, pulling her eyebrows together into a frown.

He looked at her in surprise. "*Gavin*?"

She nodded. "Yeah. Steve's actually a nice guy."

"He can be as nice as he wants," Shane said gently, "until he decides to separate Gavin from what he needs, which, in this case, is to talk to your sister."

She sat back and smiled. "In other words, Steve is no match for Gavin. Is that the idea?"

Shane nodded. "I could have pushed the issue," he said, "but I figured Gavin needed a shot. Since he and Steve are friends, I thought maybe, before it came to bloodshed or getting him fired and off the case, Gavin would let him know, in no uncertain terms, just how this would be handled."

"Oh, right. Steve's not even supposed to be close to this case, is he?"

"Nope. And this reaction here is part of the reason why. You get overprotective, and then we can't get our job done."

Looking around, she asked, "How long until that coffee gets here?"

"Not long, I wouldn't think." Almost as he said it, a knock came at the door. She hopped up, but he reached out and stepped in front of her, a finger to his lips. "I need you to stand over there," he said quietly, pointing to a corner, "so nobody knows you're here."

She frowned but followed his instructions. She listened as he went to the door and spoke to someone outside and then pushed a cart in. "Do you really think it matters if the room service staff knows I'm here or not?"

"Do you really think it matters if the kidnappers know you've escaped already or not?" he countered immediately.

She groaned. "How am I supposed to know that? I'm a scientist."

He nodded and said. "Bingo. How are we supposed to know as the good guys?"

She grinned. "You are very good at putting me in my place. Because it's what I do …"

"It's not my intent to put you in your place," he said. "I just want to keep you safe while we find your parents."

"I can't imagine what anybody would have against them," she exclaimed, at the reminder of what was really at stake.

"It's usually the simple factors."

"Control," she said immediately. "Control of the company."

"Revenge," he added in. "Consider Melinda's ex-husband and the revenge against your parents for what they did during the divorce."

She nodded. "And money, I guess, would be another one. Because they do have money," she said.

"Absolutely," he agreed, then pushed the cart toward the table.

She sighed and said, "I presume nothing alarming is in there. Like a ransom note."

"No," he said cheerfully, the cart already inspected by him. "But the kidnappers also don't know that you're here yet, so that's good."

"It is my room," she pointed out.

"Yes. And, should they find out you have escaped, they'll also find out that apparently I'm your guest." He motioned to the table. "Come on. Sit down. Let's get you some coffee. He lifted the pot and poured two mugs, placing both on the table.

She looked at the selection of tasty treats on the cart and smiled. "Now this I can handle," she said, as she reached for a muffin and a croissant.

"We can get a real meal later," he said. "I just wanted to make sure you don't crash and burn."

"This'll raise me and drop me," she said, holding up the treats.

"What do you normally eat?"

"Meat and veggies," she said. "When I eat anyway. I'm straddling both ends of the spectrum, full-out eating to none at all. I tend to get so focused on my work that I forget. So I keep a whole drawerful of power bars that I can eat if I have to."

"And how often do you have to?"

"Too often," she admitted. "I should just order in."

"You should be cooking your food," he corrected. "It's far better for you than eating out."

"I know," she said, "but that means taking extra time I don't really have."

"How many hours do you work in a day?"

She stared at him. "Too many. And obviously these questions have nothing to do with our current situation."

"You mean, with the kidnapping? Of course it does. What if people thought you were too driven and that maybe the older couple should be stepping down from the company and that you should now be the owner and CEO of the company?"

"Wow, somebody must really hate me then," she said. "Put me in a boardroom and not in a lab? That's cold."

"It's possible."

"Not likely," she said and took a big bite from her croissant.

"What about potential boyfriends or boyfriends you've turned down or snubbed?"

She shook her head.

"Dating apps?"

She just shot him a look.

He grinned. "I guess not, huh?"

She nodded. "Guess not."

"So what then?"

She shrugged. "Since my marriage broke down, I figured I didn't have the temperament for it."

"Why?"

"He always complained that I was at work."

"But didn't he know what you were like beforehand?"

"I thought so," she said, peeling back a layer of her croissant and popping the golden flaky piece into her mouth. "But, once we got married, he had these weird expectations that I would give up my job and would become a stay-at-home wife and look after him."

Shane laughed out loud at that.

She shrugged and smiled. "I know, right?"

"Gavin should really be having this conversation with you," Shane said, chuckling.

"And why is that?" she asked.

"Because you two are perfect together. He's a workaholic too."

"What does that have to do with having a conversation like this?"

Shane calmed his laughter, then smiled at her and said, "No reason, except for what I just said. You two are perfect together."

"We hardly know each other," she said, staring at him, stunned. "People just don't hook up like that."

"Unfortunately," Shane said, "they do. People hook up like that all the time."

"Not me," she said, with a shake of her head. She glanced at the door and asked, "Where is he anyway?"

"I rather imagine he's questioning your sister," Shane said. "And likely without any argument from Steve."

GAVIN KNOCKED ON the door, his rap hard and curt. He had perfected that type of knock to let people on the other side know that he would not tolerate anything but him getting his job done.

When the door opened, Steve's face immediately flashed into anger. "So what the hell is this?" he asked. "Shane sent you because we're friends?"

"Is she still sleeping?" Gavin asked.

"Of course she is," he said. "She's been through a lot."

"Wake her up," Gavin said.

Immediately fury crossed Steve's face. "No way in hell."

Gavin pulled out his phone and said, "You do it now, or I'll have you removed not only from this case but from the island."

Steve stared at him in shock. "You're not kidding me, are you?"

Gavin shook his head. "No. I have absolutely zero tolerance right now for any personal interference. You got yourself in on this detail, but, have no doubt, I will have you taken off. I'll not only have you taken off, I'll have you taken a hell of a long way away. I will talk to her, and I will talk to her now."

"Wow," Melinda said, as she stepped into the small living room. "You don't pull any punches, do you?"

He studied her face, seeing absolutely no sign of her recently sleeping. "Did you know that Shane was up here trying to talk to you a little bit ago?"

She shrugged. "I'm tired," she announced. "I wanted time to myself before I got barraged with questions."

"Got it," he said. "So it's all about you then. Absolutely nothing about your parents, who are still missing. You do realize how critical the first twenty-four hours after a kidnapping are? Correct?"

She stared at him, a feral look of animosity in the back

of her gaze.

Interesting, he thought to himself. *Now we have yet another suspect.*

"You might as well come in," she said crossly. "It's not like I'll have any peace and quiet now."

As he stepped across the threshold, Steve glared at him and said, "Don't think I'll forget this."

"Don't think I'll forget the two of you being part of this," Gavin said, his tone harsh. "Your priorities have been stated very clearly."

At that, Steve had the grace to look ashamed. But Melinda just tossed her hair. "Oh, just get over it. I'm tired. I'm cranky, and I really don't want to deal with any more of this shit."

"Fine," Gavin said. "I want to know exactly what happened from the time you left the hotel to go to the restaurant."

"Why to the restaurant?" she asked, throwing herself on the couch.

He sat across from her, pulled out his phone, put it on Record, and placed it on the table between them. She rolled her eyes, but she gave a simplified version of how they decided to go a few blocks over to a steak house because her father was a red meat eater and didn't really consider any other food a proper meal. She laughed at that. "He never was very tolerant of the dietary wishes of other people."

"So your father is arrogant and self-centered?"

She shrugged. "He's very successful, and with that comes a certain amount of ego, yes."

"So, at the restaurant, then what?"

She raised both hands in frustration. "What do you mean, *then what*? We ate. We enjoyed dinner, and then we left. On our way back, like a couple blocks, we were almost at the hotel. We were right out in front of it actually, when we were attacked," she said, and she glared at him. "It was really traumatic, you know? I don't appreciate you bothering me right now."

"The sooner I 'bother you,' as you put it, the sooner we can find out what happened to your parents."

"You should have gotten them already. I mean, we had to escape ourselves." She used such a derisive tone that even Steve winced, then sat down on the couch beside her.

"And it's awesome that you did escape," Steve said. "But your parents are older and don't have Rosalina with them."

"I guess," she said. She glared at Gavin. "You might be Steve's friend," she said, "but I don't consider you mine. So get on with whatever questions you have and then get out of here, please."

Gavin barely held back a snort. Talk about a snobby, pissed-off, self-centered female. But he did have more questions, and he worked his way through them, listening to her answers.

No, she didn't notice anything unusual at the restaurant.

No, she doesn't think they were followed.

No, she didn't recognize anybody in Honolulu that she might have known elsewhere.

No, she didn't have any idea who had done this or why.

Her answers were the same all the way down. When he was finally done, she huffed. "I told you I didn't know anything," she said, as she stood up. "Let yourself out." And, with a dismissing wave of her hand, she walked into the bedroom.

Gavin stared after her in wonder.

Steve immediately rushed in to apologize. "She is overwrought."

Gavin shot him a look and said, "Sure she is," but he got up, and he left without saying any more to Steve. Gavin wasn't sure what he was supposed to say anyway. Offering condolences didn't seem quite right. The fact that his buddy was hitching his life to that woman was enough to make Gavin question Steve's judgment. Gavin had thought Steve was a good guy, but, wow, had he ever taken a path in the wrong direction when getting engaged to Melinda.

Gavin made his way to Rosalina's room, wondering how two daughters raised by the same parents could be so different. And that sent him off on another track with a note to check DNA between them. He walked into her room to see her sitting there, munching away on a treat from the trolley in front of her, sipping a cup of coffee and conversing with Shane. Gavin realized how much easier she was to be around and how positively obnoxious her sister was. She looked up at him and smiled, and it was a genuine smile. Not something pasted on for the moment. He smiled back instinctively. "How is the coffee?"

"Excellent," she said with feeling. "How is my sister?"

He didn't answer her right away, until Shane nudged him. "Did you talk to her?"

"If you can call it talking to her, yes," he said. "Actually no. That's not a good way to describe it. I talked to her, but *did* she converse with me? No, not really."

"Oh, dear. Was she in her Royal Princess Melinda mode?"

"Oh, was she ever," he said. "I apparently disturbed her, but she hadn't been sleeping at all, by the way, Shane. That was Steve just giving her some space apparently."

Shane rolled his eyes. "Of course. No concern for her

parents?"

"No. Not only that, she went so far as to say that we hadn't contributed anything yet because these two had rescued themselves and that I should be looking to find her parents instead of bothering her."

"Lovely," Shane said, while he watched Rosalina as she shrugged and took another bite of her treat. "So, you don't like to talk about your sister?"

She shot him a look. "Doesn't do any good," she said. "Melinda is Melinda, and everybody has always given her room to develop into who she is today," she said. "You can try going against the grain, but it won't do any good."

"Interesting," Gavin murmured. He poured himself a cup of coffee, then sat back down and asked, "Do you share your sister's opinion that we're doing nothing?"

"I don't know what the hell anybody can do under these circumstances with so little to go on," she said. "I'm still trying to figure out exactly why she was gagged and I wasn't."

"So you think that's important too?" Gavin asked.

"It's an anomaly," she said, "and that makes it important."

Gavin loved that. Because she was thinking seriously like a scientist, and he agreed with her. "Your sister doesn't remember anything distinctive. Nobody followed you. Nobody may have spent too much time looking at you at the restaurant. Nothing. And yet you were obviously targeted."

"What are the chances it was random?" she countered, her gaze clear and direct. "What if they just decided to grab an older couple or all four of us on a whim?"

"Motivation?"

"Money," she said.

"And yet we haven't had a ransom demand yet."

"It's not even been twenty-four hours," she said, then stopped to look at her watch, "or has it?"

"We're pretty well there," Shane said.

"No wonder I'm hungry," she said, reaching for another muffin. Stopping, she asked, "We should have better food than this, right?"

"Yes, we should," Gavin said. "I was hoping maybe I could get your sister and Steve to join us, but, on second thought, it's probably better if we don't."

Laughing, she said, "Yeah, probably better."

"Any forensic information yet?" Shane asked.

Gavin pulled out his phone and checked and said, "I don't have any messages yet." He walked over, pulled his laptop from his bag, brought it up, and opened the chat window. He immediately asked for an update on the satellite cameras and the city cameras. Instantly two links showed up.

You could have sent those to me earlier, he typed.

They just came in. Did you question the sisters? Lennox asked.

One's cooperative. One's not. Need you to dig into Melinda's background, as deep as you can. Gavin realized he was typing the message hard and fast. **She's all about herself and doesn't give a damn about the parents, it seems anyway. Except that their loss might give her a little more attention and possibly more money. I don't know what the motivation is for the attitude. It's hard for me to understand, but it's pretty ugly.**

Ugly, ugly as in "killed her parents" ugly?

Gavin had to chuckle. Lennox knew how to cut to the chase with style. **No, ugly as in, I'm the prima donna, and everybody else needs to kowtow to me.**

Oh, one of those.

Yeah.

Also still no red flags on the exes. Back in five on the rest.

Gavin checked the two links, while Lennox was off getting information on Melinda. The links had the cameras checking all vehicles going into the parking garage and around the surface of that building, where the sisters had been held. He brought out his notepad and a pen and jotted down a couple interesting vehicles, followed them through, only to realize that they ended up going nowhere. He could spend hours doing this. Hours that these parents most likely didn't have.

He stopped and looked at Rosalina. "With your parents removed right now, does that stop something from happening at work? Or related to work?"

Her eyebrows came together as she studied him, slightly confused. "I'm not sure I understand what you mean."

But Shane did. "He's wondering if your parents had an important meeting or were scheduled to make a speech. It could be anything—a workshop, interview, presentation. Anything where their presence would be of benefit and where their inability to attend would benefit someone else."

She sat back and studied the two of them. "Well, we are here for a corporate meeting, and my father will obviously be the main speaker."

"Would it cause any kind of company instability if he didn't show, for example? Or if people found out that he'd been kidnapped?"

"Well, all bad news will affect the bottom line. That's pretty standard, I'm sure," she said. "People are generally vultures, and they'll jump ship at any sign that their money may take a hit," she said. "But this is a company board meeting."

"Wait. I thought you were here on a holiday?" Gavin stated.

"Yes," she said, "we are, but my father arranged to have several board meetings while he was here."

"So the board members are here too?"

She nodded. "Didn't they tell you that?" She looked from Gavin to Shane and back again at Gavin.

"No," Shane said, "and I spoke directly with the chairman of the board and the CFO."

Gavin pushed the notepad across in front of her and said, "I need the names, and I need them now."

She groaned and wrote in a rapid-fire movement that had both him and Shane staring at her, fascinated. Finally she was done. Throwing down the pen, she said, "I can't believe the other members of the company didn't say something the minute we all went missing."

"Maybe nobody knows," Shane said. "Were these publicized meetings?"

She shook her head. "Oh, no, mostly private meetings. He was meeting with the board of directors tomorrow and the CFO last night, I believe."

"And I know we've already asked you this," Gavin said, "but these meetings, are they unusual?"

She thought about it and said, "Potentially, yes, but I also think it's a case of my father just trying to combine work and pleasure at the same time."

"And who doesn't like to do that," Shane said.

"I understand the simplicity of my remarks. It's just a little awkward." She smiled and said, "My dad is very business oriented. My mother is not. So he probably snuck them in without telling her."

"Do you get along better with your father or your mother?"

She stared at him steadily, and he wondered what was going on behind that super-pale gaze. "Probably both about the same, I would say," she said.

But he saw no smile or any other indication that the relationship wasn't far more formal or colder than most families. He nodded, and just then Lennox came back on the chat.

Doting father and mother apparently bent over backward to make Melinda's corporate life happen. She's been in the media a lot, touted as the sweetheart of the company. She's the face of the company and has done a lot of the modeling in most of the ads. No red flags in her personal life. You already know about her divorce and custody battle, which she won.

Second sister? Gavin asked.

Never seen in the media or on the website. Not even a picture with her online biography.

"Interesting," he murmured.

"What is?" she asked.

Gavin looked up at her. "No photo in your profile on the company website."

"Why would I do that?" she asked, a coolness hitting her body language again, showing him just how much she had distanced herself from the public eye and potentially from the company.

"I guess the question is, are you connected to the company because of what you do or connected to the company because of the family?"

"Because of what I do. Haven't you figured out yet that I have very little connection to the family at all?"

"Yes," Gavin said, "and I'm wondering how that works when you're the baby of the family."

"And I already told you," she said, with a dismissive wave. "I'm not prepared to dwell on it."

"Of course not," he said. He returned his gaze to the laptop.

"Well, I don't know about the two of you," Shane said, "but I'll need to crash at some point in time, and I do need real food. So I've just placed an order for room service. Hope you like my choices. Great, if you do. If you don't, order yourself something else. After I eat, I'll go for four hours of crash time." He looked over at Gavin who nodded.

"Good idea," he said. "We need a lead. We need something."

"We need to check out the backgrounds of all the men on that list," Shane said, "but I'm presuming you've got the team on it?"

"They're tearing into the list now," Gavin said, as he finished typing the last name into the chat box. "It's a good time to get some food, then crash and burn."

"And then what do you want to do?" Shane asked.

"Honestly I want to go back to that hostage room," Gavin said. "I don't understand why no working cameras can be found anywhere around there."

"Well, there should be some on the street," she said. "All I can tell you is, I woke up in that room tied up."

"No voices in your head?"

She frowned, then closed her eyes, as if trying to remember, and shook her head. "I remember somebody had a hoarse voice, but he might have been disguising it. I don't know. When we were first kidnapped, all the voices were my mom, my sister, and my father, crying out to be let go. I don't remember hearing our kidnappers at all."

"Maybe somebody coughed?"

She thought about it. "On and off. More like clearing his throat all the time."

"Would you recognize it?"

Her eyes zipped open as she looked at him and nodded. "I don't know. Maybe but maybe not."

"Well, that's something," he said. "Smells? Was there anything in that van that you might have noticed an odor?"

"I only saw the stuff in the front of me, until they realized that my blindfold had slipped," she said. "Once they fixed that, I couldn't see anything else, and the smell was more fear and sweat."

"Male sweat?" Shane asked.

She nodded again. "Very much so."

"Like a gym socks smell?"

She thought about it and then shrugged. "Or they were scared and a little bit adrenaline rushed, by what they were doing."

"No impression on ages? Were they young, or were they old?"

"No, and yes. I did see them slightly, but they had hoods over their faces."

"How long do you think you saw without your blindfold?"

"Maybe thirty seconds before somebody noticed. No more than that for sure. The kidnapper made an exclamation sound, as if pissed, and tied it back up again."

"Did you see their hands?"

"They wore gloves. They wore black jeans and black hoodies pulled over their heads."

"Of course," he said. "So no help at all. Just what you

saw on the van."

"Which wasn't much," she said. "Sorry."

He nodded. He looked at Shane and said, "You need to sleep right away, or do you want to do a rendezvous first?"

"Rendezvous first. I want to go back there too," he said, tapping his laptop, "because of this."

Gavin leaned in and took a look.

"Black SUV at the corner."

"And why does that intrigue you?" she asked.

"Government plates," Shane said. "What was it doing there?"

"Oh, good. Good call," Gavin said. "Give me that license number." He quickly typed it into the chat and sent it to Lennox. **It was seen during the hour before the girls escaped outside that hotel. I want to know how and why and who was driving it.**

On it, Lennox said.

Just then a knock was at the door. As Shane got up to move the trolley back, Rosalina quickly filled her coffee cup and snagged the remainder of the muffins and croissants, putting them on the side table.

Gavin looked at her and said, "More food coming."

"I know," she said, 'but these will be great in case we're on the move during the night."

Damn, he loved that ready-for-anything attitude.

CHAPTER 5

ROSALINA WATCHED AS Shane took the trolley to the door and exchanged it for a full trolley with several domed plates. As soon as she was handed a platter minus the dome, she stared at the pasta and chicken with veggies on the side. "This is perfect," she said in amazement. She looked at the men's meals to see steak for both of them. "How did you know I liked pasta?"

"It came up in the bio we have on you," Shane said.

"Interesting," she said, making a face. "I'm not sure how I feel about that."

"Don't worry about it. Just makes our life a little easier when it comes to things like this, that's all."

"I guess so," she said, "but still feels kind of odd."

"No," Shane said. "It just feels invasive for a moment, until you get over it."

She laughed. "Okay, so we found a government vehicle parked outside the building where we were being held. Why is that important?"

"Maybe it isn't," Gavin noted.

"Maybe," she murmured. "Still weird."

"It is," he said.

"So what purpose is there for going to the actual site?"

"I'm tracking the vehicle now," Gavin said, between bites of food. "I want to see where it went and when it arrived." Finally he said, "Eureka."

"What?" Shane asked, looking at him.

She studied the two men with interest. They were both plowing through the food at a rapid rate; meanwhile it was obvious they were on the hunt for something on their laptops. She could feel the excitement shimmering in the air. She understood it—and approved of it at the same time— but it was a little disconcerting to see them so focused. She'd often been told that she had a similar level of focus, but she hadn't really seen it in the actions in others.

"It arrived an hour beforehand. I don't have any cameras to show that they had anybody in the vehicle with them."

"Wait. What?" she said, shaking her head. "Are you really thinking that a government vehicle dropped us off there?"

"What we need to know," Shane said, "is where the cameras for the underground parking are because that is where you would have been taken."

"Somebody must have seen something," Gavin said. He shoved the last piece of steak into his mouth and hopped up. "Time to find out exactly who and what."

She shoveled her food down as fast as she could, hating that such a great meal was not getting treated as such. But she would not be left behind. As they walked toward the door, she grabbed several of the muffins and croissants, put them in a bag before placing them in her purse, and raced after them.

At the door Gavin turned, stopped, and shook his head. "Hell no."

"Hell yes," she said. "Nonnegotiable."

"And what benefit is there," he said, putting his hands on his hips, "to having you with me?"

"I don't know," she said, "but there will be one. I promise."

He snorted at that. "No, you'll be in the way."

"I will not," she said defiantly.

He glared, but Shane laughed and said, "Come on. Let's go, or I'm leaving you both. We don't have time to debate it." And, by then, she'd locked her door and moved quickly behind them. "Do we tell the others?"

Gavin looked at her and said, "Steve picked us up. In a government vehicle."

Immediately her lips pinched together. "Do you think he's involved?"

"I have no idea," he said. "I sure hope not. I've known him for a long time."

She nodded. "I've known him for a couple years at least. He doesn't seem like the type."

"No, but you also don't know who and what might have yanked his chain."

"I don't think people yank his chain much," she said cautiously.

"Really?" he asked. "How do you see the relationship between Steve and Melinda? Because, from what I saw today, he's a man who's had his chain yanked pretty damn hard."

That shut her up. She hated to even think that Steve was involved, but the innuendo in Gavin's words meant that he also wondered if her sister was involved. Rosalina tried to be dispassionate as she thought about her sister, and Melinda's potential involvement in something like this. It was just so not her. Her sister wasn't into this level of drama or pain, but she was very much into glory. So could Melinda have twisted this into something to put her face back on the front page again? "I don't know why she would have had anything to do with this."

"She?" Shane asked, as they took the elevator down to the lower floor.

She glared at him. "If Steve is involved, then I'm automatically thinking that potentially Melinda is too."

"Oh, interesting that you would bring that up," Gavin said, "because, yeah, I did wonder."

"Of course you did," she said. "I don't know why you would have even gotten to that though. What does she get out of it?"

"That is my question to you," he said.

"I can't see that she gets anything out of it," she replied. "She's already high up in the company. She's already the apple of their eye."

"Would that have changed?"

"I don't know what you mean." She was led to a small car and given the back seat. She took it eagerly, happy to be in the background and to watch everything going on. When Gavin failed to explain, she asked him, "What do you mean by that?"

Gavin drove, but he looked at her in the rearview mirror. "Do you think there was a falling-out between your parents and your sister? Was there any reason for them to be changing Melinda's role within the company? Were they setting up a trust or something similar, and potentially she would not be getting as much as she thought she should?"

"I don't know why," she said in bewilderment. "And, if something like that were going on, I don't know anything about it."

"Are you privy to family discussions of that nature?"

"Only if they involve me," she said. "Just because I'm not the favorite doesn't mean that I'm despised or hated or not wanted."

At the men's silence, she hoped they at least understood the point she was trying to make.

"But maybe there was some recognition of an imbalance in the relationship," Shane said slowly, as he twisted around to look at her. "What are the chances that your sister wouldn't have liked that?"

"Hell no, she wouldn't have liked it," Rosalina said. "But that doesn't mean she would do something this serious about it."

"What would it take for your sister to do something serious?"

"Something like kidnap my parents?" she cried out in horror. "I can't imagine."

"Well, spend the next few minutes while we drive," Gavin invited, "and just think about it. What would be a worst-case scenario that would cause your sister to do something so drastic?"

Rosalina sat back, hating to even contemplate it. But, of course, the answer was obvious—if her parents were cutting her off. If they kicked her out of the company, and she was demoted out of the family for whatever reason. But Rosalina couldn't imagine that ever happening.

"I know what you're trying to say," she said, "but I just can't see how something like this would even be possible."

"Well, you haven't told us what we're talking about yet," Gavin said. "So what are you saying?"

"I can't imagine," she said, "that she would ever get kicked out of the family or the company."

"Interesting, but is that really what it would take?"

"Absolutely," she said, "that is what it would take."

"Okay, something to understand then."

"No," she said, "not at all. There's nothing to understand because that scenario would never happen."

They just nodded silently, sharing a quick look.

She couldn't stop shaking her head. "I don't think you understand what I'm trying to say."

"Maybe not," Gavin said, "but potentially something is there."

She shook her head harder.

"What's her relationship like with her children?"

"She loves them," Rosalina said, glad that she could at least reinforce that relationship. "She's a good mom."

"Okay," he said. "So she's a devoted mother."

"Good," Shane said. "What about as a wife?"

"No," she said, "not so much there. But I don't know all the details. I don't have the kind of relationship with her that we would talk about something like that."

"Right," he said, "but every detail, no matter how small, is important."

"I wish you would look at other suspects though."

"But your sister makes such a good one," Gavin said drily. "She's so positive and so helpful and so worried about your parents."

She winced. "When you talked to her, she was really bad, wasn't she?"

"Yes, she was. Actually she gave me a much deeper insight into what your life would have been like in the family."

"You only saw her in this mood," she said. "You haven't seen her when she's all sweet and sunshine."

"I can't even fathom that side of her. If so, she's very much a split personality, isn't she?"

"Not clinically though," she said. "I hate to say it, but there is a bit of a manipulative person inside."

Gavin snorted, and she sank back, realizing that he already understood her sister a whole lot more than most people ever did. She wondered at that. It wasn't just that her sister managed to keep the ugliness inside; her parents knew of this but never saw it. They had only ever seen the bright sunshiny child they loved and raised. They were doting parents, receiving all that sweet sunshine that Melinda had to give.

And Rosalina understood that, since she had been deemed the interloper, she hadn't seen the same sweetness from Melinda that her parents had seen. So it made for a very confusing childhood as Rosalina tried to figure out what was wrong with her. And no way to get an answer now or back then. When she realized the men were exchanging hard glances, yet nobody was talking, she leaned forward and whispered, "What's the matter?"

Shane, his voice intentionally against her ear, whispered, "Looks like we're being followed."

Before she could turn and look, he anticipated the move and grabbed her face. "Don't turn around. Listen. Stay crouched down a bit, just in case."

"Just in case, what?" she asked.

And, in that moment, the window behind her shattered.

GAVIN SWORE AS the back window exploded behind him. He quickly shifted lanes and kept on moving, his foot flat on the accelerator as he moved around and through the heavy traffic.

"That was close," Shane said cheerfully.

"Too damn close," Gavin said. "I wasn't expecting them to do something like that in the middle of traffic."

"I did get a license plate number," Shane said.

"Good. Any tracking on it yet?"

"Stolen last night apparently," he said.

Gavin just nodded because, of course, it was.

"Why would they shoot at us?" she asked, feeling surprisingly calm.

"Either to take you out or to take us out. Maybe they are afraid you saw something, heard something you shouldn't have? Maybe they are tying up loose ends?" Gavin said. "So how many enemies do you have?" She stared at him from behind the seat, and he could feel her gaze drilling into his head. But he couldn't take the time to turn to look at her.

"I didn't think I had any," she said faintly, "but this is making me reassess the situation. On the other hand, I imagine you have a lot of enemies."

He let out a bark of laughter, as he once again shifted lanes and came around the block, coming up behind where they had originally been shot. He passed the spot where the back window had exploded and asked, "Did you get caught by that at all?"

"No," she said. "I'm fine, although my hair could be a bit of a pain in the ass to clean."

"I hear you there," he said. "Hold on."

"What am I holding on for?" she asked. "Aren't you taking us back to the hotel?"

Shane smiled at her and gently said, "Of course not. We've drawn them out into the open, so we're coming around to set a trap."

Gavin laughed, unable to resist taking a look at her face in the rearview and seeing the horror on it. "You're the one who insisted on coming. Remember that," he said cheerfully.

"You guys are way too happy over this," she snapped.

"Do you realize you could have been killed?"

"We could have been," Gavin said, "but we weren't."

"But they've still got the gun," she exclaimed.

"And we're easier to spot now," Shane said, "being the ones missing the window and all."

As Shane kept working on his laptop, Gavin switched lanes and said, "Look ahead, four cars on the right."

"Quite a jam up there," he said.

Gavin nodded. "Looks like they're caught in that. And, sure enough, it looks like there may have been a bit of an accident, probably happened when they were shooting."

"So, what are you thinking?" Shane asked.

"I'm wondering about pulling off to the side here and having a talk with him," Gavin said.

"Chances are they'll get out and bail before we can get there." Shane looked at Gavin.

"Right," Gavin said, "so you first." He said, "Three, two," and, just like that, with perfect timing, Shane bolted from the passenger side, raced across the traffic, and came up to the vehicle that he suspected had shot them. It was the right license plate number. Gavin moved their car over, ignoring the horns sounding around him. Considering the early evening hour, there was traffic, more traffic than he had expected to see. "Is it always crazy busy like this at night here?"

"It's a tourist town in the peak of the season, so that would be yes," she said. "I can't believe you let Shane out like that," she said. "He could get shot."

Then she did something that really surprised him. She slipped forward between the two seats and sat in the front.

"Now you've just taken Shane's spot," he said. "So where will he go when he's trying to get away from trouble?"

She glared at him. "You're just saying that to piss me off."

He laughed. "What we're trying to do," he said, "is capture the guys who shot us. Are you telling me you don't want to know who they are?"

"Of course I do," she said, "but are we getting anywhere in all this nightmare?"

"We are," he said. "And they've just shown their hand, which means they don't want us finding anything more."

"But we didn't find out anything," she snapped.

He stayed quiet because he'd stirred the pot with both Melinda and Steve, and then this happened. He didn't know why they were behind this shooting, but it was interesting that her sister, Rosalina, was in the car that got shot at. "Any chance that your sister wasn't supposed to be there at dinner last night?"

"She wasn't coming at all on this trip," she said. "And then she decided to come with Steve and the kids."

"And what about dinner?"

"No, Dad dragged her out," she said. "The kids were not feeling well, so she planned to stay home with them, but my father wouldn't let her."

"So, in theory, she wasn't supposed to be a part of that kidnapping at all?"

Rosalina slowly turned to look at him and asked, "What are you trying to say?"

He gave her a bland look. "Maybe nothing, but maybe, just maybe," he added quietly, "the reason you two were released was because she was never supposed to be kidnapped in the first place."

"No, but then she could have been released and not me," she said, stoutly refusing to believe her sister had anything to do with this.

"True," he said, with a nod. "Quite true."

He just smiled a knowing smile.

CHAPTER 6

"I DON'T LIKE the look on your face," Rosalina said bluntly.

"A lot of people don't," he replied, equally blunt.

"You need to think about somebody other than my sister."

"I'm thinking of all kinds of people," he said. "Your sister just keeps fitting nicely into the damn role."

"She loves my parents," she said.

"Good," he said, "that would work in her favor."

"It could be Steve," she said, "but I already told you about Melinda's ex-husband. It could easily be him as well."

"And potentially still in love with her and not wanting her to get hurt. Yes," he said, "I can work with that." Rosalina sagged ever-so-slightly in place, and he laughed. "I'm not trying to fit a person to the crime," he said. "I'm trying to find the right person who did it." He pulled the car into a ground-level parking lot.

"It doesn't sound like it," she said quietly. She looked around and asked, "How come we're here?"

"Because we're about to have company," he said. A vehicle pulled up and parked in front of them. He looked at her and said, "Grab that laptop, will you? And make sure you have your purse."

She looked at him, shocked, but reached behind and

grabbed her purse, shaking it free of the shattered glass that covered it. Then she grabbed the laptop that Shane had left behind in the footwell and hopped out. Gavin walked with her, studying the top of her head.

"What's wrong?" she asked.

"Glass," he said. "Do you have a comb in that purse of yours?"

"Yes," she said. "Why?"

"Because when we get to this car right here," he said, nodding at one nearby, "I suggest you take a *quick* moment," and he emphasized that word very clearly, "and comb some of it out, so you're not transporting it everywhere."

"Is that so we don't leave a trail or for my own health?"

At that, he gave a bark of laughter. "Both."

She didn't understand him, yet wanted to, as he led her to a vehicle parked in front. She didn't even know who was inside the car. As she got closer, she bent down to see Shane holding a gun on the driver. She gasped and said, "Oh, my God."

"Comb your hair," Gavin directed her swiftly. "You do it, or I do it."

After handing over the laptop, finding her comb in her purse, she bent over and immediately ran her comb against her scalp, trying to loosen any of the glass particles. And then watched as Gavin grabbed her shirt at the shoulders and gave it a shake and then her pants.

"Are you trying to remove all trace?"

"Wouldn't that be nice," he said, "but it's not possible." Then he opened the passenger door and shuffled her in and took up a spot beside her. "We're in," he said to Shane.

"About time," he said. "Meet Henry."

"Hi, Henry," Gavin said cheerfully. "So nice to meet

you."

Henry just glared at him.

"Where'd the shooter go?" Gavin asked.

"He was already gone."

"In other words," Gavin continued, "we're sitting ducks here because the driver, the shooter, or we three will all be the next targets."

"Unfortunately quite possible," Shane said. So he nudged Henry and said, "Drive."

Immediately the vehicle pulled back out into traffic, and Henry asked, "Where do you want to go?"

"To your leader," Gavin said.

"Well, that's not happening," Henry said.

"Why not?" Shane asked.

"Because he'll kill me," he said.

"Well, one of us will. If he doesn't, I'll kill you anyway," Shane said with a laugh. "I really don't give a shit who pulls the trigger."

Henry glared at him. "No, you don't understand. He'll kill not just me but all of you as well."

"Maybe," he said, "but, at the same time, I'm wondering if you really understand where your best bet lays right now."

Gavin asked again, "Where's the shooter?"

"He took off."

"Well, of course he did, but where to?"

Henry shrugged.

"No, that's not a good-enough answer," Gavin said.

"I'm sure he's rendezvousing with the boss," Henry offered.

"And where is that?"

Henry hesitated, still weighing his options, and then said, "The shipping docks."

"Well, guess what?" Shane said. "We're up for a ride, so let's get down to the docks."

Henry shrugged and said, "It's your funeral."

"Actually it's likely to be yours."

"It'll be all of us," Henry said.

"But at least this way I know you'll go too." Shane laughed again.

Sitting beside Gavin, Rosalina had watched the interplay in amazement. "Is this some kind of a game?"

"Of course," Gavin said. "Henry doesn't want to tell us where his boss is or where the shooter went because he's trying to save his hide. Yet, when the boss finds out that Henry got taken, he's dead."

She turned to look at Henry. "I'm so sorry, Henry."

He snorted. "Why?" he asked bluntly. "Your family's behind all this."

And that set her back. She stared at Henry. "What do you mean, *my family* is behind all this? Are you saying somebody in my family is doing this?"

But Henry wouldn't be budged. He kept his lips closed, moving through the traffic like an old pro on the busy streets.

"Interesting route," she murmured to Gavin.

Gavin nodded. "I know," he said. "Backup might be required."

"I hear you." She watched in horror as they were slowly led along a much more isolated route toward the big shipyards. "I'm not sure I feel very good about this," she said. She glared at Henry. "Where are my parents?"

He shrugged.

"Why would you even take them?" she asked. "They are sick and old."

He laughed. But he didn't give her an answer.

"I don't understand what he gains by not telling us."

"He doesn't think it's worthwhile," Gavin said. "He thinks, if he can deliver us to his boss, and then can convince them that he didn't tell us anything and that we didn't get the information passed off to somebody else, that somehow he'll matter to them."

"And then he'll stay alive?" Rosalina asked.

"Well, that's what Henry figures. Of course it's all for naught because, the minute they know we've got Henry, they'll also know that he'll talk."

"I haven't said a damn thing," Henry said.

"But they don't know that," Shane said. "Yet you can bet I'll tell them everything."

"And that's just bullshit," Henry complained.

"Doesn't matter," Shane said. "They'll believe me."

Henry switched lanes and took the exit heading toward the longshoremen's area.

She shifted uneasily in the back of the vehicle.

"I told you not to come," Gavin said.

She glared at him. "Saying *I told you so* doesn't really work right now."

"Feels good though," he said, and he and Shane chuckled.

She didn't understand why they were so damn happy. Unless they already had some backup in place upfront. That would make her happy too. That they'd caught somebody involved in this was huge, though it may have been a fluke. "You know that, if your buddy hadn't shot at us," she said to Henry, "we wouldn't have caught you."

Henry shrugged.

"So this really is all your own fault. I wonder if the

shooter is dead already."

"No way," Henry said.

"Oh, yeah?" Rosalina taunted him.

"He's got to be," Shane said, picking up her gambit and rolling with it. "Otherwise he'd have already radioed ahead that you were likely coming in with us."

"He wouldn't do that," the driver said testily. "We don't tattle on each other."

"But he'd be protecting his boss right now," she said in a smooth voice. "So, therefore, it's either the boss or you. In this case it becomes the boss, so you're already out." She looked at Gavin. "They're really going to kill him, aren't they?"

He nodded, and his tone was sincere and quiet as he said, "Yes, unfortunately."

"Then let's take him back to the government offices," she said, reaching out and grabbing Gavin's hand. "I don't want someone to die."

"I get that," he said, "but, if he's not helpful, then we'll use him to get to where we need to be. So whatever'll happen will happen."

She shook her head. "If we took him to the government offices, we could interrogate him and get what we needed from him that way."

"Guys like this," Gavin said, "they don't give a shit what you say to them because they won't believe you."

She stared at him in shock. "But he's got to believe us. We just want my parents back."

"I know that, sweetheart, but he's already committed himself down this pathway, and people are counting on him. The fact that he's already been taken means that their trust was misplaced."

"Well, then he should give us everything he knows," she cried out. "To save himself."

"But he's still holding on to hope," Gavin explained. "Hope that they will believe him."

"But why would they?" she asked, feeling bewildered.

"Well, that's the trick, isn't it?" Gavin said, patting her hand gently. "Remember. You could have stayed at home."

She glared at him. "I didn't know you would put people's lives in danger."

He laughed. "Yours or his?"

She slumped back on the seat and didn't say anything because, of course, he was right. They had tried to shoot her, or maybe all of them, already.

GAVIN HAD BEEN watching the driver's facial expressions throughout the conversation, and it was interesting to see him considering his options, based on everything she said. It was a good gambit on her part, and he knew it wasn't even a trick. She truly was concerned about Henry's well-being and was wondering why he would do what he was doing.

Gavin tapped the comm in his ear to give Shane warning, as they had slowed perceptibly. Shane reached up and tapped his comm twice. They couldn't see any snipers from their vantage point in the vehicle, but it would make sense to be on the alert for them.

Gavin looked at her and said, "I want you to duck down and to stay down, no matter what happens. Do you hear me?"

When she opened her mouth to argue, he immediately grabbed her shoulder and pulled her toward him, until she lay flat on the seat. With his hand hard against her head to hold her firmly in place, he leaned over so he could look out through all the windows around them.

"What are you expecting?" she asked.

"A sniper," he said. He felt the shock go through her body and gently squeezed her shoulder. He hadn't meant to be so forceful, but sometimes you had to, to get people to sit up and to pay attention.

In this case, she found her voice in a big way. From being quiet and watchful, she now let out some of that emotion that she had been bottling up.

The vehicle kept driving forward, until it came to the large set of double metal doors of a huge hangar-looking building. Henry stopped the vehicle and said, "Well, for better or for worse, here we are."

Something about his tone Gavin didn't like. "Interesting," he said, "That's quite a gamble you've taken."

"Well, if I'm going down," he stated, "remember what I said. You're going with me." And he grinned.

Shane smiled, nodded, and said, "So hop out, and go open those doors."

Henry shrugged, exited the vehicle, stretched for a moment, and walked forward to the double doors. Just as he went to open them, a single shot was fired into the back of his head. A red spot appeared in front of him, all over the metal doors. Slowly he fell forward and slumped down.

Gavin felt another shudder rock through Rosalina.

"That was Henry dying, wasn't it?"

"It was," he said.

Shane barely opened the front passenger door, the quiet *snick* heard, and Shane said, "Give me three." And, just like that, he slammed open the door and bolted around the side of the building. Gavin checked out where the shot had come from, and he noted only one possible spot for the sniper. Part of a large loading bay where machinery with huge arms for loading were parked. Gavin had seen one man standing there.

"So, I need you to stay down," he said. "Do you understand?"

"Yes," she said faintly.

"I mean it. If somebody comes looking, make sure you look dead."

"Got it," she said.

He opened the door wide and waited while he looked to see if anybody else was up and around. When he saw no signs of anyone, he quickly slid out and dropped to his knees, his handgun up and at the ready. He wished he had a rifle, but he figured the sniper would already be long gone. It was just that kind of a scenario. Gavin headed around the same building as his partner had, knowing that Shane was already on the move.

Gavin took one look at Henry and the doors he would open, then quickly reached down, grabbed the body, and dragged it out of the way. The doors weren't locked—at least not from the outside—so Gavin counted to three and pulled one open, hiding himself behind it. Instantly gunfire erupted from inside the warehouse. He waited, and, instead of going in at full height, he dropped to the ground. He snuck around the door and saw two men standing there with handguns. Gavin quickly fired two shots, low, one for each. Both men dropped, and he ducked back behind the door.

Inside, he heard somebody roar, "You son of a bitch," as all kinds of chaos broke loose.

Gavin grinned to himself as he waited. He knew that

they would know where he was, so his position was already suspect. He studied the outside area, still seeing no signs of a sniper, and headed toward another vehicle parked down a little way. By the time he reached the safety of cover, he still saw no sign of the gunmen inside the building. He figured they'd gone around to the back.

When he heard gunfire erupt on the other side, he figured that Shane had found them, or else they'd found Shane. But Gavin didn't dare take the time to worry. He raced around to the far side, trying to find his way into the building, when he found another door that led inside. He opened it, and no more sounds of gunfire were heard. He slipped inside; it was pitch-black.

Dropping to the floor in a crouch, he searched the darkness. He was in a stairwell in a hallway. Then more gunfire erupted. He raced toward the sounds, peering through each doorway as he went. No sign of anyone. That was interesting; the area should have been busy. This was a huge port, so why wasn't this hangar active? As he came around the corner, his intercom tapped. He tapped back twice, telling Shane that Gavin was on his way.

Shane whispered, "Under fire. Four men."

"I've taken two down from the other side. Coming up inside the building."

"All handguns—still a sniper somewhere."

"On it," Gavin replied, as he came to another set of double doors, which appeared to be locked. He pulled his trusty tool kit from his wallet and quickly picked the lock, letting the door slide open just a couple inches. He could hear yelling and screaming as people shouted orders. Gavin spoke to Shane, "Are you outside?"

"Yes."

"I'm inside, coming at your six." He stepped forward as two men stood there, yelling at each other and the other two men, both barking orders, but neither was respected enough by the others to assume command. With two shots Gavin took them both out, then held his gun on the two remaining, standing there, staring at him in shock. He whispered to Shane, "Two dead, two secured. Come in slowly."

Shane stepped in through the open door on the side, then quickly disarmed the two men before knocking them both out. "That was fun," he said.

"We're still missing a man," Gavin said.

"The sniper."

Just then somebody made a noise as they tried to break free from the back of the building. Shane went after him. One of the men slowly sat up, looked over at Gavin, and asked, "What the hell?" He stared around at all the bodies and shook his head. "This is just carnage. What did you guys do?"

"You mean us or you?"

"We didn't do anything," he said.

"Funny, the handguns told a different story."

The man looked at him and frowned. "We weren't shooting at anything."

"Yes, you were," he said, "you were trying to shoot another man."

"No, we were trying to shoot the woman," he said. "We were told the woman was coming, and we needed to take her out." Then he stopped, shook his head, and winced. Apparently his brain rattled around on the inside, maybe knocking some sense into him. "No, that's not what I meant to say."

"Too damn bad," Gavin said. "You already said it."

"It's not what I meant." He reached up, cupping his

temple. "I don't feel so good." Then, sure enough, he rolled over and vomited.

"I suggest you lie down beside your buddy and stay there," Gavin said, as he searched the area, coming up and around the back and the double doors.

"Nothing's here," the gunman said, his voice kind of woozy. He laid back down beside his buddy, pointing to him. "Did you kill Johnston too?"

"No," he said. "Just the two who tried to kill me."

"That was the muscle," he said. "They were hired, but they're not us."

"Where are the captives?"

Silence.

"I asked you where the captives are."

"I'm really hoping that you're not for real," he said.

"Oh, I'm for real all right," he said. "Where the hell is the old couple? Come on already."

"An old couple was here this morning," he said. "They were removed, but we didn't know how they got here."

"Seriously?" Gavin wanted to laugh at him. But that note of confusion in the man's voice rang true.

"Yeah, when we got to work this morning, they were in the building, both of them unconscious. We called the bosses, and they came and dealt with it."

"Yeah, obviously," he said. "Where'd they take them?"

"To the hospital, man."

Gavin stopped and thought about that. Command central would have checked the hospitals and the morgues to see if the old couple had been taken there and dropped off, but nobody had confirmed with him. He'd have to ask, but it wasn't the time. "But you didn't see any ambulance, did you?"

"No, but we weren't allowed back in here."

"Were they tied up?"

"No. Like I said, they were unconscious, just lying there. We didn't have a clue how they even got in. But we've had break-ins before, so we figured that was part of it. That's why we have security around here."

"If you say so," he said.

"Look. We're not the bad guys. I can't believe you shot these men."

"Remember that part about them shooting at me?"

"Well, if you were breaking and entering, and you came in with weapons, of course."

"Remember all the gunfire a few minutes ago, before you got knocked out?"

"Yeah, they said a gang was coming in," he stated, again sounding very confused. "This isn't what we do," he said. "I'm a longshoreman. I don't deal in gunfights. I don't know what the hell's going on right now."

"Yet you had guns in your hands."

He stared down at his. "The only way that would be, is if they gave them to us in all the confusion."

"So you didn't fire it? Is that what you're saying?"

"I might have," he said honestly. "I don't even know."

"Well, you better get your story straight," Gavin said, "because they'll find GSR on your hands and your clothing."

"Well, if I was shooting, it was because everybody was," he said. And now a note of panic was in his voice.

"Ah, I see. So, when people jump off a bridge, you jump off because everybody is, right?"

"You don't understand," he said. "I thought we were in danger."

"You don't understand," Gavin said. "I was in danger."

And that shut the man up. "So now what?"

"Well, a hell of a lot of people will be coming through this place very quickly," he said. "But why is the building empty and not full of people working?"

"Well, we are working," he said, "but a strike is going on, so this corner has been shut down for today."

"Just today?"

"A couple days, I think."

"And who would have arranged that?"

"I'm not sure that I know," he said. "My head really is killing me," he said.

"Well, my buddy had to knock you out," he said, "so you didn't shoot me."

"I wouldn't have shot you."

"Well, you were standing there with a weapon in your hand, and it was turned in my direction."

"That's not who I am," he said, "honest."

"Well, I believe you," he said, "but I don't know if the cops will."

"Cops?"

"Yeah, who do you think will be handling this from here on out?" he asked. "Of course it'll be cops."

"Shit," he said. "I can't have the cops find out I'm here."

"And why is that?" he asked.

"Because the cops and I don't get along very well."

"Well, I've heard that a time or two," Gavin said. "Have you been through the rest of the building? Or even this corner? I'm not seeing anybody else here."

"No, we shouldn't have seen anybody here actually," he said. "I don't even know what's going on."

"Well, I want to believe you. I'm just not sure I can."

"Really?" he said. "Because I've never shot anybody in

my life."

"You mean, *before today*," Gavin said, and that shut up the guy for a bit.

"Did I shoot somebody?" he asked, after a long moment.

And this time Gavin could really hear the horror in his voice. "I don't know if you landed any of those shots you fired," he said. "I hope not for your sake."

"I hope not for my sake too," he whispered. "That's not somebody I want to be."

"You got a family?"

"Yeah, I do," he said, "and my wife'll leave me if she finds out about this shit."

"So why don't you tell me what the hell's going on?"

"Like I said, when we got inside, a couple was here."

"And were you supposed to be in today?"

"No," he said. "Honestly we were just sitting here and having a couple beers. We're kind of—well, the strike's really screwed us up, and the wives are pretty upset. We haven't done a whole lot of work lately, and we just wanted a place to go hang out."

"Ah." Gavin got it. "So, in other words, you weren't supposed to even be in the building, and somebody brought the kidnap victims here because it was supposed to be empty. Then you guys showed up and threw things into disarray. Is that it?"

"It sounds like that's exactly what happened," he said. "I really don't want my buddy to die either."

"Is he involved in the kidnapping?"

"Kidnapping? Kidnapping that old couple? Is that what that was? I wouldn't think so," he said. "Johnston's a good guy. He's young and has twin girls. He's got his whole life ahead of him. I don't know why he would mess it up getting involved in something like that."

"Well, sometimes that's exactly why people do things," he said, "because they need the money."

"Maybe," he said, "but I don't think he'd do that."

"So, tell me what happened when you arrived."

And the longshoreman gave Gavin the rundown about the two of them deciding to get away from their wives for a little bit and just shoot the breeze and have a couple beers. And when they got into the warehouse, they'd seen the couple and phoned the bosses. Then security had shown up.

"And they are normal security?"

"I don't know what's normal or not," he said. "I've never dealt with them before. At the same time, these men were here right away. We weren't allowed to see the couple, but they were alive. I know that."

At that, Gavin let out a gentle sigh. "Well, that's good news," he said, "because, if they weren't, things would be worse than I thought."

"Who are they?" he asked.

"A businessman and his wife," he said. "They were here in Hawaii for a visit and were kidnapped off the street."

His voice rose in horror. "Seriously?"

"Oh, yeah, I'm serious," he said. "The question is, what is your part in all this?"

"Nothing. I told you. Absolutely nothing. I wouldn't. No way."

"And yet I find you right in the middle of it all."

"And yet," said a strange voice from behind Gavin, "you're not even looking around to see who else might be involved."

Gavin slowly turned to see a man with a rifle over his shoulder and a handgun in his hand, currently held against

Rosalina's head. "Oh, interesting," he said. "That worked out really well, didn't it?" Rosalina just glared at him. He smiled at her reassuringly.

"Oh, I don't think so," the man said. "No more of your tricks."

"What tricks?" Gavin asked. "By the way, is this guy telling the truth?" Gavin pointed to the one conscious guy on the floor. "Does he have anything to do with you guys?"

"Why would I tell you that?" the sniper asked in disgust.

"See what happens," Rosalina said to Gavin, in a biting voice, "when you leave me alone?"

Gavin laughed. "Remember that part about, you weren't supposed to come with us?"

"Well, it's a good thing she did," the gunman said. "Saves me a trip later."

"Interesting," Gavin said, "so she really is one of the targets."

"Sure," he said.

"What about the other sister?" But the sniper just shrugged. "She's not though, is she?" he asked. The sniper again just shrugged.

"We were both released," she said, with a gasp. "Why do you keep harping on Melinda?"

"Oh, no reason," Gavin said, with a smile, wondering how long Shane would be. But just then, Shane's voice came in a whisper through Gavin's earpiece.

"Keep him busy. I'm two minutes away."

"Are you sure you don't want to tell me how this is all supposed to work?" he asked the sniper.

The man stared. "I don't give a shit how it's supposed to work or if you know or not," he said. "I'm too much of a professional for that."

Gavin studied him, taking a closer look. "Mercenary?"

"Hell no," he said. "Contractor."

Gavin wanted to laugh. "There's a difference?"

"Absolutely there is," he snapped. "I pick and choose my bosses," he said.

"Well, that makes a hell of a difference, doesn't it?" he said with seriousness. Because he did understand that people had problems with bosses all the time.

"Absolutely it makes a difference," he sneered.

"And your boss this time?"

"What about him?"

"Must be good money, huh?"

"Not the greatest but it's getting there," he said. "As you should know, it takes time."

"As I should know?" Gavin repeated.

"Yeah, I know who you are. And your buddy. You all think you're some hotshot military special ops guys. But you're not. You're just the same as the rest of us hired guns."

"Well, I don't think anybody working for Uncle Sam considers themselves a hired gun," Gavin said slowly.

"No difference," he said. "Same damn shit only, like I said, I get to pick my bosses."

"So, you were in the navy?"

"I was," he said, "but I wasn't part of all that rah-rah bullshit."

"Not a team player, huh?"

"Not that kind of team player," he said with a snap.

At the same time, Rosalina stared at Gavin, waiting.

Gavin liked that about her; she was very observant and understood that things were going on around her that she didn't understand, but, rather than questioning and making judgments, she was waiting. And so was he.

"Now, I want you to move forward," the sniper said to Rosalina. "Nice and easy."

"Sure," she said. "Anything you say. You've got the gun."

"You better believe it," he said.

"Where are my parents?"

"They're safe," he said calmly.

"Good," she said, "but where are they?"

"Well, we obviously had to move them," he said, "but, like I said, they're okay."

"I want proof."

"Well, bitch, it doesn't matter what you want," the sniper said with a laugh. "Because you're not the one calling the shots."

"So who is?" she asked him in bewilderment. "What could my parents have possibly done to deserve this?"

He laughed. "Nobody ever expects who it'll be when they find out they've been betrayed."

Unfortunately that was so very damn true, Gavin thought to himself.

"Is it my family?" she whispered. "I don't see myself getting out of this unscathed," she said. "So I would really like to know who I can thank for this predicament."

"Well, I don't know. I'd have to get an okay from the boss before I tell you anything," he said. "I haven't been paid yet for everything, so I want to make sure there are no issues in that quarter."

"I see," she said quietly. "How about a hint. I won't tell."

"Sure," he said. "It's somebody close to you. But not likely somebody you would think of."

CHAPTER 7

S OMEBODY CLOSE? WELL, that would certainly fit her sister, but was the sniper saying that? Was she letting words taint her thought process? As a scientist, Rosalina could read nuances. She could utilize something here. If she could figure out the data, surely something in this situation would make sense if she applied her brain to it. "That could be all kinds of people," she said slowly.

"And they thought you were so smart," he said, laughing. "That's the thing about those you never see."

"*I* never see?"

"Exactly," he said. "Like I said, it's not somebody you would ever expect it to be."

Now she was stumped, and, of course, all she could do was think about everybody in her world. "But why my parents?" she asked. "They're harmless."

"Hardly," he said. "They're very wealthy, and they hold a lot of power in their hands, power that they're not choosing to wield in the way that this person thinks they should."

"Ah," she said, "so somebody who is pissed off at them."

"Not necessarily," he said, "but it's not like the boss talks to me."

"Right. Back to the boss again," she said, her tone derisive. "A boss you said you got to choose."

"Well, I took on the job," he said, with a laugh.

"And what about the rest of your buddies, like Henry?"

"Yeah, see? Henry was not supposed to get caught. For that he would go down anyway."

"Interesting," she said. "So does the person live here?"

"Nope, just has ties here," he said. "Of course that's likely to be what gets him caught, but he doesn't seem to think so."

She latched on to the *he* with relief. "So it's not my sister! Thank God for that."

He laughed. "Wow, so much sisterly love. To actually consider that shows just how much you do understand her. She's not a very nice person, but you could still be wrong on your assumption."

GAVIN NEEDED TO be ready for anything because he knew Shane was right here; he could see his shadow. But they needed a diversion. With the gun held against Rosalina's head, it was just way too close for comfort.

"Well, it is kind of sad," Gavin said, "to see a family torn apart like this."

"Yep, and it's all about power and greed and positions and all that good stuff," the sniper said with a smirk. "Nobody is ever happy enough with what they've got."

"I'm not surprised," Gavin said. "As you and I both know, that's what makes the world go around."

"Well, it certainly keeps us employed," the sniper said.

"And what about these guys here?" Gavin asked, motioning at the longshoremen, lying here in stunned shock on the ground, pretending to be unconscious, if not one of the two already dead.

"Yeah, they didn't have anything to do with the kidnapping," the sniper said, "but I can't leave any of them alive, of course."

"Yeah, of course," Gavin said casually. He noted the shock, the imperceptible reactive movement of the guy he'd been speaking with earlier. "On the other hand, you don't really have a reason to kill them, since they're out cold anyway."

"Maybe," he said. "Maybe not."

Just then a loud *bang* rang off to the side, where several old barrels were stored.

The sniper looked over and smiled. "I suppose that's your partner trying to cause a diversion, huh? It won't work, you know." He fired off a couple shots in the direction of the barrels. "There. We'll just let him think that it worked."

"Ah, we don't have to think about it," Shane said, as he placed his handgun against the sniper's head.

He froze. "Shit," he said. "Where did you come from?"

"Think about a diversion. It's really only helpful if you're in a position to make good use of it," Shane said. "So I set it to crash a few minutes after I left the area, so I could already be here." As he spoke, he quickly grabbed the sniper's wrists and disarmed him. "So now," he said, "we'll have another talk, only our way." Grabbing the man's hands, he pulled him forward.

Freed, Rosalina raced to Gavin's side, where he opened his arms and tucked her up close. "What the hell?" she whispered. "This is one messed-up world."

"Oh, it is," Gavin said, "but the good news is that now we have the sniper."

"Does that mean he'll be dead soon, like Henry?" she asked.

"Possibly," he said, "but this is the guy who killed Henry."

She looked at the gunman and frowned. "Why would you do that?" she asked. "Henry was a nice guy."

He laughed at her. "A nice guy he was not. He just had that beautiful unassuming air that led a lot of people to be deceived as to who he really was. Same as other people. If you look into a supposed break-in here in town, you'll see that a mother and daughter were shot before breakfast, and that wasn't random at all. The husband was responsible for that one."

She stared at him in shock. "Why would you take a contract like that?"

He looked at her and asked, "What do you do for a living?"

"I research ways to make people's lives better," she said, simplifying it.

He laughed and said, "Well, so do I. The husband's life is infinitely better without those two bitches in it."

She shook her head. "That's cold."

"Yep," he said, "but it's also the way of the world."

"It isn't if it's not what you want," she said.

"Well, it is the way I like it," he stated. "I tried the navy and got out as fast as I could," he said. "That was so not my style."

"That's because you don't like following orders, and you're not a team player," she scolded him.

He just shot her a hard look.

Behind the sniper, Shane laughed and said, "It doesn't do any good to try to stop her."

"Doesn't matter," the sniper said. "You can take me down to the cops, and I'll be out in no time."

"Why is that?" Gavin asked.

"Because I don't have anything to do with anything," he said. "I just happened to walk into this area and saw a dead man at the front door, and I came in to help the poor longshoremen," he said. "And look what I found. Two gunmen."

"Right," Gavin said. "Like that'll work for you."

He shrugged. "Why not?" he said. "It's your word against mine. And I'm a local. You're foreigners."

She smiled. "Maybe, but my father's got a lot of money. And he donates a lot of it. And money talks and not just to get people killed."

"You've got to find him first," he said, laughing.

As they walked him out the front doors where Henry had been shot, she stopped and said, "You know what? I don't feel very good going out there."

"I know," Gavin said. He looked at Shane.

His partner shrugged and said, "We got to take him back."

"I suggest we call for backup," Gavin said. They stood just beside the open door.

Shane looked at Gavin, then at the sniper, and asked, "You think he'll talk?"

"No." Gavin really didn't think so.

"WE CAN'T LET him go," Rosalina said, "but I don't want you or him to get shot if you lead him out of here either."

"Well, let's tie up his feet too, and we'll just leave him inside the door," Gavin suggested, as he and Shane trussed up their captive, pushing him to the ground. "We do have men coming, but I also need to make sure that longshore-man back there is okay."

She looked at him and asked, "Who?"

"One of the two men Shane knocked out earlier." He looked at Shane and said, "Keep an eye on her." And he turned and bolted backward. She stared at the sniper on the ground, catching a twitch of his lips.

"It's a trap," she gasped out to Shane. "Oh, God, Gavin's gone into a trap." Then she turned and bolted backward. She could hear Shane calling her to come back, but it was too late. As she got into the area, she stepped in behind the stacks of boxes occupying one portion of the room and watched as Gavin reached down to check on the two unconscious men. Just then one pulled his hand out from beneath him, holding a handgun, and held it against Gavin's head.

"Shit," she whispered. She looked around but saw no weapons on the floor.

Gavin slowly straightened as the other guy moved to get up, but Gavin's knee came up and slammed the gunman in the jaw, as Gavin reached for the gunman's hand and snapped it backward. While the longshoreman screamed in agony, the gun went flying, his arm hung loose, completely snapped.

She stepped out and stared at him.

He looked over at her. "What are you doing here?" He frowned.

"Well, I figured out it was a trap," she said simply, "so I came to help." She held her hands wide and said, "But apparently you didn't need it."

He beamed at her. "Maybe not," he said, "but thanks for the thought."

GAVIN STARED AT Rosalina, trying to figure her out. She was the one who had been kidnapped, but she was right there at all times, trying to help. There wasn't much she could do, but the fact that she'd even come after him had said a lot about her character. Sure it was foolish and had put her in unnecessary danger, but she hadn't necessarily known he was looking for a trap. She'd only been thinking about him walking into one. He looked down at the man, sobbing at his feet. "We need to get a cleaning crew in here," he said. "A lot will be involved."

"And they won't be very happy about it," she said quietly. "Are you sure you don't want to call Steve?"

He shot her a look and shook his head. "We'll keep Steve out of the loop, but we've got people coming."

"How do you know?"

"Because I trust Shane," he said, with a smile. And, sure enough, in the distance, he could hear emergency vehicles coming. He reached down and grabbed the injured man by the back of his collar, lifted him to his feet, and prepared to join the others. Gavin's weapon was now holstered in his back waistband, and he marched his captive to where Shane was.

Shane raised his eyebrows when he saw him. "So, a trap?"

"Well, he definitely pulled a gun on me," Gavin said. "The question is whether he really understood what he was doing or not."

"Of course I didn't," the man blubbered. "I thought you were coming back to kill me."

"Right," Gavin said, completely not believing him.

At that, even Rosalina laughed and said, "Then no need to try to kill him, was there?"

"I didn't know who was who," he pleaded. "I was lying there, with my eyes closed. You didn't have to break my arm."

"You didn't have to try to kill me," Gavin said, giving him a shove so he ended up heading toward Shane, who moved the longshoreman ahead and out of the building. From there they stood and watched as the government vehicles piled in around them. Several men came forward, frowns on their faces. Gavin understood because nobody liked to see anybody on their side that they didn't know and didn't understand. All these secret government departments that nobody wanted to keep a secret, but it didn't change the fact that sometimes the local authorities needed the assistance of these secret entities. He gave a brief report and explained what was going on and then said, "Now we're leaving."

One of the men protested. "We'll need a lot more information than you've provided here."

"Then you can call me," he said, calmly leading Rosalina to the vehicle. "And make sure you actually have questions and aren't wasting my time."

One of the men snorted and said, "Fucking spies."

Gavin stopped. Turned. "Well, I better not have heard what you just said." Gavin's gaze was hard and direct. "I guess you guys have forgotten what team we're on and who almost got shot up in there."

They just glared at him.

"Yeah, I thought so," Gavin snapped. He hopped into the driver's side, his nerves already needing an outlet. With Rosalina in the back seat and Shane beside him, Gavin backed up, turned around, and pulled away. "They never change, do they?" he muttered.

Shane shook his head. "Of course not. But, if you were on their side, dealing with the everyday secret stuff going on in a city this size, and then in comes something even more secret, you'd be pissed too."

"I guess," Gavin said, relaxing. "I tend to forget that, even though we're on the same side, different levels are here and everywhere."

"I don't understand any of it," Rosalina said from the back. "Why the cloak-and-dagger stuff anyway?"

"Because the locals have rules," he said. "They are bound by certain restrictions that we aren't. So we have more leeway to get the job done."

"You snapped his arm, like it was a twig," she muttered.

"Well, it was either that," he said, "or have my head explode, like a melon. I prefer the twig analogy."

Shane nodded. "A good point," he agreed. "We can go in there, and we can raise Cain and all kinds of hell, but we still have to protect ourselves. We're not here to hurt civilians. We're not here to hurt anybody—other than bad guys who are putting guns to our heads," he said, by way of explanation.

Gavin thought it fell far short of what all they did, but, as long as it kept Rosalina happy, he was good.

"So, what do we even know now after all this?" she asked.

Gavin looked at Shane, but he was busy on his phone. "Make sure we get cameras of this area from the time they were all kidnapped to this morning, when Rosalina's parents were moved."

"Yeah, looking for the links now," he said. "Got to be

some cameras around this place."

"Why would they bring my parents here?" Rosalina asked.

"I would ask you the same question," Gavin said, as he pulled into traffic. "Most likely it was an empty location that wouldn't link to them."

"Right. I don't think they have any relationship at all with the docks," she said. "It's not like we're importing and exporting anything."

"Maybe not," he said, "but you never really understand what kind of businesses people are in."

"Well, you can say that again," she said. "I definitely don't. I'm all about the research."

"And who would be all about the ordering, shipping, and receiving?" he asked quietly, looking at her in the rearview mirror. She stared up at him, her eyes darker than he'd seen them before. He figured it was stress fatigue or even the nightmare of what she'd just seen.

She shrugged. "We have a purchaser, or buyer, whatever you want to call him. So I guess him. But I don't know that he does anything other than handle the mundane stuff of getting more test tubes and pencils," she said in exasperation. "For the level of something like this, it would be much more. It has to be much bigger than that."

"So, you tell me," Gavin said. "This is your company. This is your field. What would make it bigger?"

She sank back against the upholstery and turned her face to stare out the window.

But he could see the wheels churning in the back of her brain. It was a fascinating process. He never really thought that superintelligence would appeal to him, and he wasn't sure that was the draw here as much as how it was packaged and how she utilized it. He loved the fact that she was straight to the point, honest, and up-front. And he really had to like somebody willing to come to his rescue. As ill-equipped as she may have been and whether he needed it or not, still she came. He didn't think she was the kind to jump after lame ducks in the world, but she'd certainly jumped after him.

"I can't imagine," she said. "We didn't need any more investment money," she said. "We were approached, I believe, by a couple companies who wanted to invest, but my father declined."

"Well, that could be interesting," Shane said, twisting in his seat to look at her. "Do you remember who they were?"

She shook her head. "No. I don't think I was ever even told directly. Just something I heard being discussed."

"Who would be discussing that kind of stuff?"

"Employees discuss everything," she said drily. "Whether they know anything about a topic or not. Honestly it's one of the reasons I keep to my little corner. Because there we can keep the discussions to science."

"Instead of really boring stuff, like management, financial analysis, and all that, huh?" Shane teased.

"Okay, so maybe I've led a far-too-simplistic life," she said, "but I'm following my passion and am happy doing it. Supposedly other competent people were taking care of the rest of it. And, if that is their passion, all the more power to them," she said. "I don't want to feel guilty for doing the stuff that I do."

"I agree totally," Gavin said smoothly. "But some of these discussions may very well be pertinent to what's going on right now."

"Maybe," she said, "or maybe it's got nothing to do with

it."

"Won't know until we find out," he said. "So, who would know?"

"Well, my father of course," she said, "but, then again, so would my sister."

"Did you have nothing to do with the business side of it?"

She shook her head. "No," she said, "nothing."

"Did you show up for the shareholders' meetings?"

She stared at him in horror. "You've got to be kidding. Have you seen those things? No way. Dad forced me to go when I was assigned my shares, and I showed up. It was nothing but a zoo of pasty-faced people, lying through their teeth, yet smiling, as if they were best of friends. No, not my kind of deal at all."

"Wow," Shane said. "They aren't all that bad."

"Well, that's the only memory I have of the one time I went," she said. "It's enough to keep me away forever."

"Well, it's enough to use as an excuse to keep you away forever," Gavin said.

At that, she broke into a laugh. "True enough," she said. "It was ten years ago, and I don't even know if the board members are the same people I met back then."

"Not likely," he said. "And, if you think about it, they would probably be different people anyway, just because of the number of years that have passed."

"True enough, but, at the same time, I can't see spending my time dealing with that kind of political gerrymandering on purpose."

"Understood," Gavin said. "Shane, did we get back much on any of the board members?"

Shane shook his head. "Nothing interesting. Background

stuff and contact numbers."

"You're not calling them, are you? We have to keep this quiet," she said, horrified.

"What do you care if the whole world knows what happened to your parents?" Gavin asked, his tone taking on an edge. "Surely you want us to do anything we can to get them back safe."

"But how will involving more of the company keep them safe?" she asked, staring at him in the rearview mirror.

"I don't know," he said. "How will it hurt them?"

"Because, if somebody in the company is involved," she snapped, "they might just decide to kill my parents, so they can't tell what's happened to them."

"Exactly," Gavin said, with a smile. "Which is why we probably won't talk to anybody, but I was hoping there might be somebody you thought was trustworthy."

"They are people," she said. "That makes them all snakes."

CHAPTER 8

ROSALINA WAS STILL struck by the swift simplicity and ease with which Gavin had snapped that man's arm. Even as the guy had been led away, clutching his arm and bawling his eyes out, Gavin had appeared completely unaffected. She didn't know if that was just a requisite for the work he did, and he really was unaffected, or if it was a mechanism that helped him to keep his sanity when regularly dealing with the kind of violence he was exposed to. She understood the need for force at times but still found it shocking, up close and personal like that.

So far they still had no clue what had happened to her parents, yet they were closer, she admitted to herself. The fact that her parents had been at that hangar was huge. Now what they needed was forensics to explain who else was there. Surely somebody had to have known something. Between the dead men and those who were left, she wasn't sure anybody did though. At least not anybody still left to speak.

And how absolutely distressing was it that so much was going on in this world right now. She was getting a little more worn down every time she heard of more. She'd insisted on coming, but, now in the dark, she wondered what was next. She leaned forward and asked, "Are we going back to the hotel?"

Shane nodded. "You and Gavin are," he said. "I'm going

to police headquarters and see if I can get any information out of our prisoners."

"And I'll," Gavin said, "research their backgrounds."

"Do you really think they'll talk?" she asked.

"I'm hoping the one will talk to me," Shane said. "It's not like I broke his arm." He ended it with a smile on his face.

"So it should probably be me," Gavin said, "because he'll know I'll break his other arm."

She realized he probably would too. "I wish the violence wasn't necessary," she said quietly.

"Right," he said. "In that case maybe you should stay at the hotel for sure because this is the kind of world we're living in right now."

"I know that. I'm not a child, and I realize we use violence to get answers from violent people. I just wish that wasn't needed."

"Understood." They took several more corners, and the hotel loomed in front of them. She felt such a sense of relief to know that they could hopefully put the nightmarish outing behind them.

As she stepped from the car, she said, "I guess I'm really looking forward to grabbing some sleep. Just a few moments to step out of this craziness."

Gavin grabbed her arm gently and nudged her toward the front doors. "We'll get that right now."

But, even as she watched, Shane exited the passenger side, hopped into the driver's side, and took off. She stared after him, confused. "Shouldn't you be going with him?"

"Nope," Gavin said, as he hooked his arm a little more securely with hers, bringing her gaze to his, and urged her through the double glass doors that opened automatically in front of them.

"What if he's in danger?" she asked, twisting to look behind at the disappearing car.

"Well, thank you very much for being concerned," Gavin said, as he led her toward the elevators. "But, at this point in time, this is what needs to happen."

"I don't need looking after," she said slowly, searching his face, wondering if that was the reason for sending Shane off alone.

"So says you." Gavin tapped the elevator button that would take them to the third floor, where her room was. As soon as the door opened, he checked the hallway and led her to her room. There he held out his hand, and she gave him the key. He opened the door but entered first, with a finger to his lips, and left her at the open doorway. She frowned, realizing what he was looking for and half expecting to see an intruder in there. He did a quick pass through her room, then brought her in.

Checking the hotel hallway again, he locked the door behind her. She moved into the room and noted the trolley was still here with their dishes. She quickly packed it up, setting aside the sweet desserts and adding them to the stash of croissants and muffins she pulled from her purse. Now that she was back to relative safety again, and, although she might very well need some more food, she wasn't sure she could get anything down with her stomach as upset as it was. Gavin pushed the cart back outside, and she didn't see what he did, but he was gone a bit longer than it took to just put it out in the hallway. When he reentered, she stared at him. "Where did you put the cart?"

"Out in the hallway but a few doors down. We don't really need anybody to know that we're here."

"Security cameras?"

He smiled, shook his head, and said, "I fixed the one on this floor before we came off the elevator."

She sighed. "Is everything so easily hackable these days?"

"Unfortunately," he said, "it's all so-too-easily hackable. That's the way of the world right now."

"Well, it sucks." She sagged at the end of the bed and gave her face a scrub with her palms. "I need sleep," she announced. "My brain is fuzzy."

"Do you want a shower first?"

She shook her head and, walking to her dresser, pulled out her pajamas. "No," she said. "I just need to rest." She went into the bathroom and, after a few minutes, came out with her robe around her and slipped into bed, tossing away the robe, and curling up under the blankets. "Are you staying all night?"

"I sure am," he said.

She looked over at the table and saw that he'd cleared it off and already had added his laptop, papers, and something else, maybe a tablet or a phone beside him. Yawning, she asked, "How can you just keep going?"

"I need to," he said. "You know the kidnappers won't give a shit about sleeping."

Immediately she felt guilty for getting some sleep. "Why haven't they contacted us?"

"Because they don't want anything from you," he said, his gaze piercing her in the half light. "This isn't about you. It's about them."

"If they don't want anything from us, meaning like a power move or money, what could they possibly want from my parents?"

"Information—or for them to do something that they

don't need anybody else's signatures for."

At that, she slowly sat up and said, "You mean, like change their will or sell shares?"

"Sign contracts," he said. "Make agreements under duress. Sign confessions."

She stared at him. "My poor parents."

"Agreements made under duress aren't legal under the law," he said, "which would require your parents to fight it afterward, unless the threat was big enough that they wouldn't for fear of the threat being acted upon."

"Meaning that, they could be killed if they tried to fight it?"

"Most parents don't give a crap," he said, "but, if a threat were made to kill you or your sister—"

"They would cave in immediately," she said, nodding. "It's who they are."

"I get that," he said. "And, for that reason alone, they've probably picked up your parents as part of the process to get to the end of what they need done."

"But, if they gave somebody shares, and it was under duress, and my parents couldn't fight it afterward, surely somebody else could do something to stop it."

"To remove the threat, you have to remove the threatened end result," he said, "usually going after the people behind it. So, for example, say somebody wanted control of your family's company and needed to redistribute shares for control of the company. They become this new dark horse, somebody put into power in a company."

"Sure," she said, "but it's written down that my parents can't do that without giving the two of us the first option to buy all the shares."

"But that's spelled out in their Last Wills and Testaments, right? As an inheritance?"

She nodded slowly. "Yes, their shares are to be divided evenly between the two of us."

"So, what if your parents were just killed outright, not changing their current wills?" he asked quietly. "Who then has enough shares to take over the company?"

"Well, nothing would change because my sister and I would vote the same."

"Is your sister heavily involved in the shareholders' meetings?"

"Yes, she is," Rosalina said slowly, not wanting to go in that direction, with her sister deemed guilty.

"And, if you're not here," he said, "who will get your inherited shares?"

She immediately pressed her lips together.

He nodded slowly. "Your sister does, right?"

Rosalina took a slow, long, deep breath. "Yes," she said, "my sister does."

"Making your sister a very wealthy, very powerful woman in the company."

"I still think you're wrong," she said, sliding deeper into the blanket and curling back up again.

"No," he said. "You don't think I'm wrong. You *hope* I'm wrong," he said, "and that's an entirely different thing. You are very intelligent. Put that brainpower of yours to work and look at your sister. Look at everybody around your sister. Figure out if this is something she would do or could do. Don't just go on feelings."

"Normally I never have feelings to go on," she muttered.

"That's because you've kept yourself so strapped down. You've kept all that emotion rolling underneath that hard shell of yours to the extent that you've never really been allowed to express it."

"You don't know me that well," she said. "You can't say something like that."

"Sweetheart, I know you better than you know yourself," he said ever-so-gently. "You were that child who wasn't loved, in your viewpoint. You were the spare, but, since you were perfect, it served only to highlight how much the child they really loved was damaged and just showed how much more help she needed."

Rosalina couldn't stop the sob that choked the back of her throat at his words.

"Your childhood would have been nothing but catch-up, trying to prove to your parents that you were worthy of their love. And nothing you did was ever good enough in your opinion because nothing you did ever made you feel like they loved you the same as they did Melinda. Which is true. They loved her because of her disabilities. They loved you because of your abilities. Different kinds of love but both are love, in your parents' own ways. So it wasn't a competition. You didn't want it to be, yet you couldn't stop trying to reach for the same thing. If we were in any other scenario, and I didn't know who you were," he said, "you would be my prime suspect, the one who looks the most guilty in all this."

"Seriously?" She sat up straight.

He looked at her and smiled. "Who is the one who gains the most if your parents go?"

"We already went over this," she said. "The two of us."

"And your sister's already been through an ugly divorce. She's got another marriage happening, and she's frustrated and frightened. The world sees her as *less than*, doesn't it? So your parents have given her an awful lot more support, and I wouldn't be at all surprised, if and when you see the actual share division, you will find that they've given her a little bit more."

"Well, maybe they have," she said, "but I don't need the shares."

"But the world expects you to react like everybody else, and that means you would want those shares. So, maybe you're the one who's angry. Maybe you kidnapped your parents to make them change their wills."

"But I would never do that," she cried out.

"I know that, and you know that, but that doesn't mean anybody else knows that."

"You're just grasping at straws," she muttered, flopping herself back on the bed and staring up at the ceiling. "It was tough growing up," she murmured. She'd been quiet for a long couple moments thinking about the lonely nights she had stayed in her room, while her parents sat with her sister, who was tormented by nightmares.

"You became self-sufficient, capable, and independent because you didn't have a choice. The more you did so, your parents realized just how much you could do without them, and they backed off even further, right?"

She nodded slowly. "I don't think they did it on purpose though," she whispered.

"No, of course not. They were parents, and they needed to split up their time as equitably as they could," he said. "And, with one child needing so much more of their care, obviously the other child would either learn to thrive as an independent or would suffer and would end up with a condition or mental instability that demanded the parents give them more attention. You chose to go the other route and isolated yourself, becoming stronger and stronger."

"Not so strong, if you can see that inner child so clearly," she said. His analysis was very invasive, and yet he wasn't doing it in a way to hurt her. He just stated the facts, and she appreciated that because facts were what she was comfortable dealing in.

"When you realize that you'll never get the same love from your parents as your sister, you convince yourself that you didn't need it in the first place," she said. She thought of all the hours she had spent at school plays or assemblies, getting awards upon awards, just hoping to see her proud parents in the audience, only to find their spots were empty. Because her sister would have needed the hospital or another of her PT sessions.

And, if it came down to her sister's ballet lessons or Rosalina herself getting an award, her parents would smile and tell Rosalina that she'd get another award. Then it would be hands down Melinda's dance lessons. These were just the facts of Rosalina's childhood world, and she'd long since gotten used to it. Until Gavin sat there at the table with that well-intentioned, smooth-talking voice and brought all these little bits and pieces out of the shadows and into the light. She didn't like what she saw.

"Was she always manipulative then?"

"Always," Rosalina said sadly. "She sees her disability as something that makes her so much less. Thus her insecurity is so vast and deep that she requires everybody to give her so much more, all in order to fill up that well of insecurity. But she's really a nice person when you get to know her."

Gavin gave a bark of laughter at that. "Well, I haven't seen that side of her," he said. "The person I met wasn't somebody I would choose to spend any time with."

"I know, right? Nobody ever sees that better side of

Melinda, who she is with my parents," she said, laughing. "When she wants to be, she can be very nice. I have seen it at times."

"Was she actively hateful toward you?"

"Oh no," Rosalina said. "Distant and cold. Calculating, as if trying to discover how she could make me look worse and herself look better. I think that's a safeguard of any child, just trying to make the world happen for themselves. I don't blame the young girl she was."

"No, of course not. Because you're right. Every child tries to manipulate their environment to make their situation the best it can be," he said. "So, no, I don't blame the child at all. But you can certainly take a closer look at the adult and realize how much better she could have been. If you get to blame anybody, blame that version of Melinda."

"You see? That's the difference between me and the rest of the world," Rosalina said, as she rolled over to look at him with a small smile. "I don't have the time or the energy to blame anyone. I just moved on and found a passion, and that's where I spend all my time and effort."

"And I bet that alone," he said, "probably made her even angrier."

She nodded, pulling the covers up to her chest. Closing her eyes, she whispered, "Yes, it definitely did." She heard the note of satisfaction in her voice that she couldn't even begin to contain as she let herself drift off to sleep.

ROSALINA CONTINUALLY AMAZED him. Not only was she always willing to see her sister in a better light but Rosalina was also willing to avoid blaming anybody for her childhood and her life growing up. It was an interesting combination of personalities that she presented. She hid behind her intelligence. Those busy eyes of hers seemed to see everything—yet only as she looked outward. She refused to look inward.

Maybe because the pain was so intense or maybe because she already knew what was inside and felt it was lacking. Either way, she fascinated him. She dozed gently on the bed, not even six feet away. He had shifted so that he could keep an eye on her, to make sure any nightmares didn't overwhelm her while he worked on the laptop.

He'd been given the link to the vehicles coming and going from the warehouse. According to the cameras, a nine-minute glitch started at 1:15 p.m. this afternoon. A vehicle had come in; the two people had been dropped off, and the vehicle had left again. But having a glitch like that just meant Gavin now had a specific time. A place to start searching for the vehicles that came through the nearby busy intersections.

It didn't take him long to narrow it down to a small green van. Not new, not necessarily old, but a fairly nondescript delivery van. One similar in size and shape to the one that had kidnapped the four of them in the first place. So, where had this van been in the meantime? Zooming in, he managed to get a license plate number, which he quickly put into the chat box with his orders. And then he kept looking to see where it traveled next. He managed to track it across most of the city, at least the downtown core, where it disappeared into a massive parking structure. He waited, keeping track of the vehicles coming and going. The green van didn't leave for another seven hours.

He frowned, typed the address into the chat box, and wanted to know who owned it and were there any living accommodations inside. Now Gavin watched as the green van headed up and went in the opposite direction from where the couple had been left. So, had Rosalina's parents been there in the warehouse that whole time? Maybe it was a delivery job? The parents were picked up from wherever they had been originally stashed and removed to the warehouse, and then the delivery person went home for the night? So the next day was a whole different business day, potentially onto his own world? Whatever that was.

Gavin thought about what the one longshoreman had said—the one who had pulled a gun on Gavin. So these guys couldn't be trusted as to anything they had said earlier. And no cameras were in the warehouse, which also made him pause. Who would know how many cameras and where the cameras were located if they weren't involved? Unless somebody hadn't given a damn and just cut the electronics. If you cut the electricity and took out the security line and the internet feed, that was an easy way to make sure you got everything disabled.

But, if her parents were just lying there, unconscious on the floor, tied up, that meant somebody had taken them from the van, carried them in, and left them for somebody else to pick up later. And yet, by the time Henry had driven them there, the parents were already missing. So somebody else had come and picked up the parents and had taken them away before all hell had broken loose.

Gavin kept searching for another vehicle that would have removed the parents from the warehouse property. And it really pissed him off when he realized it was less than an hour before he had arrived. He caught sight of a black truck with a canopy leaving the docks that he hadn't seen any-where along the area. It had gone in the direction of the right warehouse, but then Gavin had lost track of it.

When it showed up again, it was driving slowly, but Gavin had no way to know what or who was inside it. However, with the license plate number, he could hopefully track it down. As he dropped that one into the chat box, he got the green van's license plate data from Lennox.

Plates are stolen. Need more details on the vehicle if you can. I presume it wasn't a black truck?

Small green delivery van. Gavin quickly went back and took a screenshot and popped it in.

So the license plates were stolen, but that didn't mean the vehicle was. Pretty easily, anyone could switch license plates. People often thought that was the best way to throw off the police. But they didn't realize that the police often had methods of finding out whose vehicle it was anyway. Gavin went back to searching for the black truck on the traffic cam feeds. Then he brought up an image of it and added it to the chat box. **Need to know where this one is too.**

Those are the license plates for a van.

Maybe for the green one I saw earlier? So they switched both plates?

Yes. Immediately came an address, name, and picture ID of the person who had it insured.

Gavin noted it was an older woman, maybe in her late seventies. He checked for a birthdate and soon confirmed she was seventy-nine. **Well, she wasn't likely driving it herself**, Gavin entered.

Lennox popped up and said he'd run a history on her family and friends.

Gavin replied and asked for more information on the black truck, telling Lennox it may have been the vehicle that took away the couple.

It belongs to Johnston's mother. Lennox confirmed and the chat box disappeared.

Gavin studied the information in front of him on the woman. A little more research came up with the fact that she was a longtime resident, had type 2 diabetes, and used to be a schoolteacher. She had retired a good twenty years earlier. That explained the purse and sweater in the vehicle.

"Good for you," he said, "a life well lived and hopefully a retirement well enjoyed."

He kept muttering to himself as he worked his way through the rest of the camera feeds, trying to find images of the sides of that truck as it left. He had a search set up, and images flashed constantly, as the computer went from one camera to another, until finally Gavin saw the black truck leaving the outskirts on the north side of town. He switched to a satellite feed to see if he could pick up anything on it.

And then it headed into another town, where Gavin switched to street cameras again. Then he caught sight of the canopied black truck driving into a long driveway among a bunch of trees. Then it stopped. He took note of the address and popped that into the chat window, then looked at his watch to see what time it was, as a road trip was about to happen.

But he wouldn't leave Rosalina alone. Neither could he trust Steve and Melinda. As much as Gavin wanted to think the family could stick together until he cleared the other two from some involvement in the kidnappings—which at the moment he sure as hell could not—he wouldn't leave Rosalina alone or with those two. He texted Shane, who replied, and they shared a quick exchange. **Where are you?**

On the way back to the hotel.
Good.

Why?
Road trip.
What about Rosalina?
No idea. Suggestions?
Take her with us.
Not sure that's a good idea.
Leaving her behind is a worse one.

Gavin sat back and stared as he contemplated that because really it was a simple case of just the two options. They took her with them, or they left her behind. But, if leaving her behind would put her in danger, then the better option was to take her along. He could also put an armed guard on her, but that might piss her off, and there wasn't any guarantee that she'd be any safer, particularly if the guard had anything to do with Steve.

Gavin didn't want to think his old friend was up to no good, but Gavin had seen it happen time and time again. So he just didn't trust Steve enough in this situation, especially where he had personal stakes involved. Ten minutes later a rap came on the door, so he got up and let Shane in.

"Where are we going?" Shane asked, as he threw a bunch of gear into his bag.

"I saw a green van leave from the warehouse, about the time of that 1:15 p.m. glitch, probably when the parents were first taken to the warehouse. But then, about an hour before Henry brought us there, a canopied black truck left the longshore area, probably with the parents inside. I tracked him from Oahu to the north side and up to the next little town, where they've turned in to a long driveway up on the far side."

"Oh, good," he said.

"Not necessarily because I couldn't confirm that anybody was in the back between the smoked windows and the overhead canopy."

Shane stood with his hands on his hips as he thought about it. "And, of course, no cameras were around the warehouse building."

"Exactly. Cameras were there but have been smashed. The van that delivered them had stolen license plates, from the black truck with the canopy. So the license plates had been switched."

"What we need then is to find that black SUV from the crime scene."

Gavin gave a bark of laughter. "Believe it or not, the cops are on it."

"They should be on all this, but are they?"

"If they aren't, we are," he said, "so it doesn't really matter. Is anybody getting upset with us?"

"Only like today, when we show up somewhere and leave dead bodies behind."

"Right. I figured. How did the interviewing go?" Gavin asked Shane.

"The guy with the bum arm, thanks to you, clammed up as soon as he got medical treatment," Shane said. "He's not willing to talk. We have his name and his ID, his rap sheet and his list of known associates," he said, "which I shared with the chat window, but it doesn't mean necessarily a whole lot yet."

"Good," Gavin said, "it's something at least."

"I didn't waste my time on the sniper. I knew he wouldn't be talking. What we still need though is something a whole lot more than this."

"That's why I want to take a look at this country property," Gavin said. "I figure we'll take about an hour to run up, take a quick look around, and then an hour's run back. And, of course, we'll still have communication with the Mavericks chat box, if anything pops up."

"And what's likely at this point?"

"Well, we can always hope that something breaks."

"Are we leaving her?" Shane asked.

"No, you are not," she said from under the covers, her voice sleepy.

Gavin walked over and sat down beside her. "We'll go do some reconnaissance where a particular vehicle has parked."

She sat up slowly. "Give me a moment," she said. "I'll get dressed and join you." And, with a little more vim and vigor than he expected when she was still half asleep, she hopped from bed, snagged her clothing, and walked into the bathroom.

He raised his eyebrows at Shane, who just shrugged. "It's probably better if we stick together anyway."

"Unless we're walking into danger ourselves," Gavin replied.

"I know, but let's not look at it like that."

"Got it," he said with a grin.

Back out of the bathroom a few moments later, Rosalina was completely dressed, with her face washed and her hair pulled back. Grabbing her sweater, putting on her shoes, and snagging her purse, she said, "I'm ready."

Gavin led the way without a sound, locking up the door behind her. Instead of taking them through the main part of the hotel, he dropped down into the car park, and he slipped into a vehicle right in front of them.

"Different vehicle," she murmured quietly from behind him.

"Well, one of them had a broken window," Gavin said

with a smile, "and the other one was borrowed from Henry."

"I wonder what the legal term for *borrowed* is in this instance," she said.

He chuckled. "Not sure. We can look that up."

"Right," she said. "Where are we going?" He gave her the name of the town. She brought it up on her phone and asked, "Why would they go there?"

"Close to town but far enough out of the big city. Personally, if I had to work in Oahu, I'd be finding a place out of the city to live myself."

"A lot of commuting then," she muttered.

"Depends on how often I'd have to come in," he said. "I would much prefer to have a couple acres and live a few miles away."

"Not everybody can afford a couple acres," she said, with a laugh.

"Maybe not," he said, "but I've spent so much of my life in the city jungles that I'd just as soon retire from all that."

She sat back and stared at him through the rearview mirror. He smiled at her and said, "Don't worry about it. Just keep on looking at whatever you're looking at."

"No, but it's an interesting insight," she said. "What about you, Shane? Are you leaving the city when you're done too?"

"Possibly," he said. "Depends on what *done* will actually mean though."

"Meaning, whether you do or do not survive long enough to retire?"

Gavin could hear the joke in her voice, but it was definitely an attempt to hide some of the negative aspects of their work.

"It's always possible," Shane said.

"What about you?" Gavin asked her.

"I don't know," she said. "I've spent so much time in the lab that I tend to forget there's anything but that."

"Right," he said. "Work can be all-consuming, and then we have nothing left at retirement."

"Exactly," she said, as they drove steadily out of town. "Any chance we can stop to pick up a cup of coffee?" she asked. "I know it's not a sightseeing trip, but I could use it to wake up."

"Yes, of course," Gavin said. "Do you need food too?"

She shrugged. "I should have brought some of those muffins and croissants that were still left."

"Not necessarily," he said. "I think we've got them." He looked over at Shane, lifting a bag from the seat beside him. "Yes, they're here," he said.

She crowed lightly in the back seat. "Now that is awesome," she said. "I'm really glad to see that."

"At least it's something."

"It's a lot of something."

Gavin pulled into the nearest coffee shop drive-through and ordered three coffees. He looked at her. "Do you need anything in it?"

"No," she said. "I like my coffee black."

"Good enough." When they were given the take-out cups, he paid for it and proceeded to pull from the drive-through.

"You don't worry about your face being caught on any of the cameras?" she asked.

"Not at this point," he said. "We're just having a drive."

"Yeah, but it's the direction we're going," she said. "Surely that makes a difference."

"It does," he said, "but not that much."

"Awesome." She accepted the cup of coffee from Shane, then gave him a smile and reached for the bag. As he watched, she snagged a muffin and proceeded to settle into her seat.

"Do you always eat this much?" Shane asked.

She nodded. "I used to put it down to the fact that I have a really fast metabolism," she said, "but now I've pretty well figured out that it's due to my brain constantly moving. Do you know that professional chess players need thousands and thousands of calories over and beyond the normal person?"

"I hadn't heard that," Gavin said. "But that would assume then that brainpower is a high-calorie energy requirement."

"It is," she said with a nod. "And I never really put the two together, but, when I'm researching, I tend to be hungry," she said. "After all, I'm constantly calculating and working on data, running scenarios in my head, looking for anything to make it all work."

"Which is kind of nice," he said.

"It is," she admitted, as she held up the last bite of her muffin. "Besides, it lets me eat. And I really like my groceries."

He chuckled at that. His gaze caught sight of a vehicle behind them. He glanced at Shane to see him studying his side mirror. "Can you catch the numbers?"

Shane shook his head. "Not yet."

"Okay, let me slow down a bit and see if we can get him to come up behind us." He maneuvered into the slow lane, even though it was nighttime, and the highway through town was pretty well empty. As the vehicle came closer, it slowed down and pulled behind him again. "Not very smooth there," he said.

"Not smooth at all," Shane said.

"Okay, you guys are scaring me. What's going on?" she called from the back seat.

"We're being followed," he said, "but it's not a pro."

"And I suppose that, once again, I'm not allowed to turn around and look, right?"

"Right," he said. "And I think you should slink down a little bit, just in case I decide to shoot out the back window."

She gasped and immediately sagged down so she was flat on the seat. She had her coffee in her hand. Shane looked around and said, "That does not look comfortable."

"No shit," she glared at him. "Do I need to be like this?"

"Well, you definitely should have your head below the seat back," he said, "but there's got to be a more comfortable way to arrange yourself."

She shrugged, then shifted, so she lay on her side, using her purse and sweater as a pillow, still holding her coffee cup. "It's just awkward drinking coffee this way."

"Well, don't spill it," he said. "It's damn hot."

"I know," she said. "But still, it is what it is."

"True," he said.

Gavin listened to it all with only half an ear. As he watched the vehicle stay just enough behind that he couldn't really see into the vehicle. "We should have a zoom lens so we could get a closer view."

"Better than that," Shane said, "I'm trying to get the chat window to check it on satellite, to see if they can get any more details than we have."

"Good idea," he said, as they exited the city limits and headed up the stretch of highway. "It'll be interesting to see if they make a move," he said.

Immediately Shane brought up the map of where they were going. "If they do," he said, "I'm thinking it'll be eleven miles ahead. Looks like a turnoff's on the right."

"I can make that work," Gavin said, his mind already thinking about a play to get out of the way.

"The question is whether it's just the one vehicle," Shane said.

"Well, let's keep our eyes open for a second," he said. "I can hit the gas pedal to the floor, but I don't know this road."

"We're doing just fine right now," Shane said, "as long as they stay behind us."

Gavin drove on for the next ten miles, realizing they were coming up on the city within a few miles. "No move yet, and we need to pull off here in a couple miles, but I don't want them to know where."

"The turnoff's up ahead," Shane said. "Instead of slowing down, why don't you hit the gas and go as fast as you can, then tuck into it as they speed up."

Gavin laughed. "I love it." And that's what he did. He pressed the pedal to the metal and sped ahead, going faster and faster and faster. He looked for advance notice of the turnoff, happy to see a little dip in the road that should keep them out of sight for a bit.

Meanwhile, as the vehicle sped up behind him, trying to keep up. At the last minute Gavin hit the brakes hard and tucked into the turnoff on the same side of the road. The vehicle flew past at high speed and hit its brakes, but it was already too late, and the people following them were well and truly past. With no other options than turn around or keep going, they kept on going.

Gavin killed the lights and waited, watching as the follow car's red taillights disappeared over the horizon.

CHAPTER 9

S HE WATCHED THE men work in awe. She leaned
forward and whispered, "Is it safe now?"

"It's safe in that you can sit up, yes," Gavin said. He
took the lid off his coffee as he studied the horizon. "The
question now will be if they come back."

"But, if they do turn around and come back," she said,
"won't they see us?"

He nodded. "If we stay here, they will." He pointed to a
grove of trees up to the side where it was flat and level. "So,
I'll probably pull in there, and we'll give it a few minutes."

"Interesting that they came that close, actually letting us
see them," Shane said. "So was that on purpose? Or just not
pros?"

Gavin looked at his partner. "Cops?"

"That's what I was thinking. Or one of Steve's navy
buddies? FBI? Or hired locals?"

"As in Steve hired them?" she asked in shock. "Or the
same department?"

"Could be either," Gavin said. "Could be local hires, like
at the warehouse."

She watched as he put the lid back on his coffee, put it
down, and, without turning the lights back on, moved the
vehicle across the road and pulled it up into the shadows of
the tree growth there. She wasn't even sure what type of

tropical foliage it was, but he managed to tuck under a bunch of long leaves. "Is it even safe to park here?"

"Well, there's no hill, and it's flat," he said, "so it looks safe enough to me." And just then headlights came down the road, facing them.

"But how can you tell if it's them or not?"

"We can't," he said. "At least not yet."

The vehicle slowed as it got to the turnoff and kept on driving past.

"Well, that's them for sure," Shane said, "and I got the first three digits."

"I got to the last three," Gavin said. Shane quickly wrote it down, and she watched as Gavin texted it to somebody.

"Are you still thinking government?"

"It's hard to say," Gavin said. "Things like that can get misconstrued very easily."

"Not to mention that sometimes government vehicles get used on private jobs," Shane said. "So you can't always blame the government, even if it's a government vehicle."

She was a little nonplussed at that. "Do you think they'll turn around again?"

"They'll either think they lost us or that we turned around and chose a different route," he said. "With any luck they'll head that way for another few miles before they come back in this direction again, in which case we need to be long gone." They sat here and waited in the silence while Gavin watched in the rearview mirror.

She kept looking, but the highway stretched for a long distance behind them. When the car completely disappeared from sight, Gavin started the engine, turned on his lights, and pulled out. "How far is this place we're going?"

"Not far at all," he said. "Maybe ten minutes to the

turnoff, which is why we wanted to make sure they didn't know where we were going."

He kept driving for the next few minutes, while she watched and studied the area. The sun was just crossing the horizon, giving a much lighter air to the world around her. It was almost a magical moment, with the tropical ocean in the distance and the colorful wildlife and such lush greenery all around. It was really special. Yet the reason she was here was the opposite, but she still noted the stunning scenery. "Has anybody checked in with my sister yet?"

"No. Why would I?" Gavin asked. "I talked to her yesterday, and that was plenty."

"She doesn't know about our parents being at that warehouse then, does she?"

"I didn't give her an update, but that doesn't mean that somebody else didn't tell her."

She sagged back and wondered if she should.

"I wouldn't if I were you," Gavin said.

She glared at him. "You're not allowed to read my thoughts now too," she snapped.

"Then stop thinking so loud," he said with a chuckle.

In spite of herself she smiled. She was really comfortable around very few people, but he was definitely one of them and getting more so every moment. She didn't have a ton of friends. And she certainly hadn't dated at all in the last few years. Her marriage had been cold, and she thought that trying once was enough to know it wasn't her thing. But apparently it wasn't, as now she truly hated never having somebody there for her.

And what she hadn't realized early enough was that the coldness of her marriage meant her husband had been looking for heat elsewhere. It had really bothered her to find out he'd cheated on her all that time. He had said he assumed she'd wanted an open marriage since she was gone all the time anyway. There hadn't even been any recriminations when they divorced, more just wondering why they had bothered in the first place.

Rosalina watched as Gavin slowed the car and didn't even signal before he took a road off the main highway.

"So do you just not know how to use signals," she asked, "or did you do that deliberately?"

"Deliberately," he said. "Just because we can't see anybody watching us doesn't mean they aren't."

"Don't you think they'll see the vehicle as it turns up here?"

"Probably," he said, "but you don't want to give people enough warning to let them know ahead of time that this is what we're planning on doing." Instead of continuing up the drive, he pulled into another heavily green area and parked, shutting off the engine. He looked back at her and frowned.

She gave him a frown right back. "What's that about?" she asked.

"Just trying to decide what to do with you."

She groaned. "Why don't I just lie here with the doors locked, while you guys go do your thing?"

"I like that idea," he said. "A blanket or something should be back there to cover yourself with. Make sure it's thrown over you so nobody can see your face."

"Am I trying to hide then?"

He nodded. "Absolutely."

She sighed, then searched around, and there, on the floor in the other footwell, was a blanket. She didn't have a clue how clean it was, and it didn't seem to matter to anybody else. She fluffed it out and threw it over the top of her, pulling it up to her neck.

"Remember what I said about your face," he said. "Your skin will shine in this light."

Surprised, she sank under it.

"Much better, thank you." He reached over and patted her gently. "We'll be back as soon as we can."

Just then the doors closed and locked, and the two men disappeared. Even though she listened very hard, she couldn't hear their footsteps recede. How did that work? How did they possibly slide through the night so quietly like they did? She knew he'd just say *training*, but it was more. It was a sense of oneness, a sense of rightness. It was a sense of coming together with this atmosphere and this earth at this very moment in time and becoming one with it all. They didn't disturb anything, they just moved with it.

She didn't shift her body, for fear of somebody noticing her movement. And yet that was stupid. Still, there was only so much she could do. She lay still and quiet as she waited for them to come back. And waited.

And waited.

And waited. And then she started to fret. She hadn't heard anything. No sounds of gunfire, no voices. Nothing. So where the hell were they?

THEY'D ALREADY CIRCLED the house once, before breaking in and doing a quick search of all three floors—basement, ground level, and second floor, even the tiny attic—finding no signs of life on the inside. No sign that anybody was at home in any way, shape, or form. Gavin was looking for the black truck with the canopy he'd seen arriving here earlier on the satellite feeds, but, from the ground, everything looked much different than from above.

He couldn't find a vehicle parked anywhere, but another property was close by that was easy to miss with the tree canopy, but, even after searching the outside of that second house, Gavin found no sign of the black truck. However, he did find a three-car garage attached to that house. And he desperately wanted into that. Even with his best efforts, every time he tried to shift the door, the squeaks let him know it would groan loudly if he pulled it open more. And that meant he couldn't take the chance.

With Shane sliding through the darkness at his side, they crept up to the kitchen to find the door unlocked. They stepped inside, listening for sounds of anybody around, but there was nothing. Instead of searching the house, he headed straight to the garage access. And there, with the door opened, Gavin stepped inside. Using his phone as a flashlight, he checked the vehicle in the middle and found it was the one he'd been tracking.

He turned, gave Shane a thumbs-up symbol, and then went to the back of the black truck and checked to make sure it was empty. No sign of anyone was there, but Gavin found a purse, several gags, and a sweater. He pulled the purse toward him and checked it out. Sammie Johnston, the wife of one of the guys knocked out at the warehouse perhaps.

He nodded and said in a low whisper, "Well, this is definitely the truck that had Rosalina's parents." He left the purse and took several photographs for evidence and sent them to Lennox, along with the license plate and the location of where they were at. Then they went inside, looking for the parents. They had to be somewhere; Gavin just didn't know where.

Inside the second house, they quickly searched the main floor, but it was empty and cold, as if nobody had lived here. They swept upstairs, guns at the ready, and checked out each and every bedroom but found nothing. He and Shane stared at each other in the hallway, as they contemplated their options.

Then he looked up and frowned at the handle to the attic. Shane studied it, nodded, and gave him a three-finger countdown. When they reached one, Gavin dropped the door, and Shane bolted up top. And again found nothing.

Gavin was right behind him, his handgun up, only to find the attic space empty as well. "Shit," he whispered.

"They have to be somewhere," Shane whispered back.

"Unless they were moved elsewhere that we didn't see," he said.

"Did the vehicle stop anywhere on the way here?"

"No," he said. He holstered his weapon and sent a message to Lennox to bring forensics in here, even though they still had no bodies, alive or dead.

"They have to be here then," Shane said softly.

Gavin made his way back down the attic stairs again. "Let's check for a basement. I mean, it's possible that he met somebody on the road, and there was a glitch in the camera system. It's possible that he pulled up in traffic and made a switch. I don't know," he said.

"Yeah, but all of that would mean taking too big a risk," Shane said. "The easy answer is, they're here."

"And does that mean we need cadaver dogs, I wonder," Gavin said. "I hope not because that would really wreck Rosalina."

"I wonder if it would wreck Melinda," Shane said.

"*Humph.* Not likely."

With one quick dash around the main floor again, they searched for a basement and found access at the back of the pantry. Gavin went first and quietly crept down the stairs. He wished for a light but didn't want to turn one on and get hit with a bullet. Just too damn easy in a case like this to get shot.

As soon as he could see below, he stopped and crouched for a moment, waiting for the shapes to make sense to his eyes as they adjusted to the darkness. Boxes. Wood. All kinds of just junk. He silently crept down the rest of the stairs. With Shane right behind him and his phone up as a flashlight, he quickly did a preliminary search.

On the post at the bottom of the stairs was a light fixture. He looked at it, checked around, and then hit the switch. Instantly a glaring white light lit the overstuffed basement that had been long forgotten. It didn't look promising, but then Gavin grabbed Shane's shoulder and pointed at footsteps in the dust on the floor.

He nodded, and they each crouched behind the boxes. The footsteps only went in one direction and didn't return. That meant somebody was down here. Checking around the boxes quietly, waiting for a bullet to come their way, the two men finally made it to the last corner, not finding anything, just the tracks leading away from the stairs.

Gavin stopped. The trail ended right at the wall. He stared at it, then at the footsteps in the dust on the floor, looked all around for a secret door, then shook his head and whispered, "What the hell?"

"Another room has to be here," Shane said.

They studied this wall, looking for something, their fingers pressing, seeking a hidden mechanism. It ended up being on Gavin's side, and, as he pressed in one spot, he heard a tiny *snap*. The two looked at each other, and the door opened silently.

There were no lights on, so, with flashlights confirming that the footprints once again went inside, Shane slowly ducked into what appeared to be almost a hallway—a tunnel—and realized they were heading back to the neighbor's house. Shane smiled.

They made their way through the long tunnel—at least twenty feet long, connecting the two homes—ending at another door on the other end. Before Shane pushed and tried to open it, he held his ear against it, listening for any kind of sound, and there it was, ... voices. He listened intently and held up two fingers, then a third. Three people were on the other side of that door.

He looked at Gavin, both of them pulling out their weapons again, and, when they were ready, Shane grabbed the door, shoved it open, and called out, "Hands up!"

CHAPTER 10

"**W**HERE ARE THEY?" she snapped, now getting irritated. She shuffled under the blanket, feeling hot and sweaty. She pulled it back after she rolled over, so she lay face down. But it was morning out there, so her face surely couldn't make any difference now. Not only that, her bladder screamed for relief. She wondered how mad Gavin would be at her if she got out, but she didn't have a whole lot of choice. She pushed the door open on her side, then slid out and walked a few steps.

Crouching behind the back of the vehicle, she relieved herself. Not the best answer and certainly not one she would choose, but one's basic physical needs must come first. When she was done, she grabbed a couple napkins she had had for the muffins, and, when she'd cleaned up, she stood ever-so-slowly and looked around the vehicle. She saw no sign of the men at all, no sign of life for that matter. Nothing was out here.

She studied the area, not having a clue how many people lived up here, but she could see a couple houses in front, and the road continued farther up and on past. Maybe more homes were up there, but it wasn't obvious from the gravel road. No major tire tracks because the gravel was still fairly loose. And, of course, that meant absolutely nothing, and, for all she knew, a huge subdivision was up there that people hadn't yet moved into.

She groaned softly, enjoying the fresh breeze now that she was out of the vehicle. She didn't want to make any further noises, so she couldn't shut the door, but she pushed it almost closed and settled down into the trees. She'd see the men if they came, and she'd see anybody else as well.

When her phone buzzed, she pulled it out, hoping it was Gavin or Shane, but instead it was her sister. Her sister at this early hour of the morning? Her sister sent her a text message.

Do you want to meet for breakfast? I can't sleep, and I know we haven't talked, and we need to.

Rosalina thought about it, frowned, and realized she certainly couldn't meet for breakfast anytime soon. She sent back a message. **Trying to sleep. Maybe later.**

Eight?

We'll see.

Downstairs hotel restaurant?

Yes.

Okay. And sorry, sis.

Rosalina sent back multiple question marks. Then typed, **Sorry about what?**

But Melinda didn't answer.

Ten minutes later, Rosalina heard a branch crack behind her. She whirled around to see a man standing there, holding a handgun on her. He gave her a big wide happy smile.

"I knew you'd be somewhere close," he said.

She stared at him in shock. "What are you talking about?"

He said, "Hand over your phone. You're not contacting anybody."

She hated to, but, given that he had the upper hand, she didn't have much choice. She held it out, and he put it in his pocket. She stared at her lifeline to the outside world. "Why do you need it? What are you doing?"

"I'm taking you somewhere," he said, his joy a little too hard to contain. He grabbed her by the arm and moved her up to the front of the vehicle.

"Where are you taking me?" she asked, trying to resist.

"Look. If you'll keep struggling," he said, "I'll just knock you out and throw you over my shoulder."

He was a mountain of a man, and she believed he would do that easily enough.

"Fine," she said, "please don't hurt me."

"I won't if I don't have to," he said. "I'm not into beating up women."

"Says you," she said resentfully. "It appears you are into making them do things they don't want to do though, so what's the difference?"

He glared at her, his smile falling away. "I don't hurt women," he said. "Other people do, and I have to follow orders sometimes, but that's not my problem."

She took a deep breath, trying to figure out that convoluted logic. "So, you'll hurt women if you're ordered to, but, other than that, you wouldn't do it by choice."

"Well, I would just as soon not do it at all," he said, "but sometimes I don't get that choice."

She nodded ever-so-slowly. "Well, you could just let me go," she said. "I haven't done anything to hurt anybody."

"Maybe," he said. "But somebody sure seems to think you have."

"I haven't," she cried out. "I spend all my time in the labs."

"Maybe so. Doesn't matter to me," he said.

"But you just said it does." She tried logic, but there was

no getting through to this guy. He appeared to be a whole lot of brawn and a little short on brains. He held himself to an honorable standard, yet was completely swayed by what other people told him to do. He led her up to the house and forced her inside. She stopped to look around, but it was empty, with no sign of anyone.

"What will you do to me?" she asked, allowing some of the fear holding her in check to seep out. "Please don't hurt me."

He shrugged, then pushed her down on the couch. "Just sit there."

She sat there, quietly curled up in the corner as she watched him. He paced, as if waiting for something to happen. "What are you waiting for?" she asked.

"You'll find out soon enough," he said. And she was afraid it wouldn't be anything she wanted. He had a gun, but he didn't appear to be keeping it on her. She studied the room. There was a bunch of older furniture in floral patterns. Floral in every direction, in fact, but there was a window in front and the front door. Then, as she twisted around, she could see a fireplace and a dining room behind her. She presumed a door was at the back wall, but that didn't mean that she would reach it before he caught her.

The advantage of being small and slim was that she was fleet of foot. He, on the other hand, was big and bulky, and she could only hope that he wasn't a linebacker who could run fast too. The front door was a whole lot closer, but she still had to get away from the line of bullets, should he shoot to stop her. And that wouldn't be easy. She looked at him. "How long do we have to wait?"

He just shot her a look. "The longer it is, the better for you."

At that, she took several deep, slow breaths and said, "But I haven't done anything to anyone."

"And again, that doesn't matter," he said.

"So, is this all about being in the wrong place at the wrong time?"

He shrugged. "I don't have a clue. And what it's about doesn't matter to me."

"Meaning that you have a paycheck coming, and nothing'll get in the way of that," she said, bitterly hating how the world worked.

"Yeah, that's about it," he said. "Hey, I've got a family to feed."

She studied him for a long moment. "You've got kids?"

He nodded. "Yep," he said. "I got two boys and another one on the way."

"So, of course you need extra money for that."

"And how." He snorted. "Nobody ever tells you about the real cost behind kids."

"What will you do when you have a girl?"

"Be a proud papa," he said, that grin of his splitting and lighting up the room.

She studied him for a long moment. "Yeah, you're a proud papa, until somebody down the road decides that your daughter's a pawn and that she should be snuffed out just because somebody says so."

Immediately he spun and stared at her in horror.

"What? Do you think I'm not someone's daughter?"

"Maybe," he said, forcibly pulling himself backward. "But I can't let it matter."

"And why is that?"

"The pay. It's too big," he said. "So sorry. You're it."

And she realized that there really wouldn't be a happy

ending to this. If she escaped from the room and from the kidnappers, she thought that maybe she would get out of this hole. But she seemed destined to go from the frying pan into the fire in this situation. "I was kind of hoping," she said, "that you would see reason."

"Too much at stake," he said.

"Right," she nodded and smiled. "Well, I hope you enjoy your money when you realize that your daughter will be the one to pay the karmic price for this."

"*Pfft!* Karma's a bitch, right. Except she's not real," he snapped.

"Right. Well, I know for a fact that it's definitely real."

He totally ignored her.

She tried again. "Whatever you do, early in your adult life, tends to come back on your kids."

"That just goes to show you that karma's not real," he said. "Why the hell would anybody go after my daughter because of things I've done?"

"Well, maybe you should ask yourself why anybody would go after me for something I didn't do? It's all apparently because of something somebody else did."

He stared at her for a long moment and then shrugged and said, "We'll deal with it at the time," he said, "but I'll kill anybody who tries to hurt my daughter."

"Your mythical daughter," she said. "What if somebody hurts your wife while she's carrying your daughter?"

Again he rounded on her. "Is that a threat?" His voice rose to thunderous proportions.

She gave him a bland expression. "Do you really think people won't be looking for me? People who are coming to help me? What happens if they go after your wife as a way to get me back?"

He shook his head. "They have to find her first," he said.

"Well, that should be easy enough," she said. "These guys can find anybody."

"But they don't know who I am," he said, as if she was simple.

"But they will," she said, "and you better believe it."

"Why? Are they some kind of Secret Service?" he scoffed. "As if those guys know anything. They can't find anything without help."

"Maybe," she said, "but I highly doubt that they'll be stupid about it. And, although you haven't touched anything," she said, "you know there's hair transfer. There's DNA evidence all over."

He looked around, looked at his jacket, and shook his head. "You're just trying to scare me."

"I'm trying to warn you," she said. "Now that you've taken me," she said, "you've crossed a line."

He glared at her. "I don't like being threatened."

"No?" she said. "Neither do I but what the hell. Apparently I've just been kidnapped a second time now."

"You weren't supposed to escape," he said, at least confirming that he was part of the same kidnapping.

"How could I possibly not escape? she asked. "It was actually pretty damn easy. And why the hell was my sister gagged, and I wasn't?"

"I don't know," he said.

"You're not the one who tied me up? Or did you kill him?"

He shook his head. "I only heard that you escaped afterward."

"Bully for you. Then what happened to the guy who tied us up?"

He stopped, looked at her, and said, "We don't kill people for that."

"You mean, for letting a prisoner escape?"

He shook his head. "It wasn't his fault."

"And whose fault was it?" she asked him, suddenly trying to get into his mind-set and to figure out just what kind of logic this guy was operating on.

"He was new. It was his boss's fault for not checking your ties."

"How do you know that he didn't check them though?" she asked.

He looked at her again and said, "Well, it's easy for you to say that, but he can't defend himself now."

With a sinking feeling, she realized that the man who had checked her bonds was now dead. "So the supervisor was killed but not the ineffectual employee?"

"Everybody has to learn," he said.

"So, if I escape from you, would you get killed?"

He nodded. "Probably, which is why you're not escaping because that's not happening."

She nodded slowly. "It would be a shame for your kids to not know their father," she said.

His gaze narrowed at her. "That won't happen."

"I'm afraid," she said, "that it is. Definitely."

He walked forward, his weapon out. "I can just blow apart your knees," he said. "That'll stop you from escaping."

"Yes," she said. "It will. But it won't do a damn bit of good to stop the men who will vindicate my death or the injuries you inflict on me."

For the first time he looked a little nervous.

She nodded. "You should be nervous," she whispered, "because they're coming."

"Unless they're already captured," he said with a big grin. "Just because you think you know something doesn't mean you know anything."

She laughed. "And here that should be my line."

He glared at her. "Just stop talking," he said.

"Yep," she said. "I can do that."

He pointed the gun in her direction again, letting her know *no more* talking would be allowed.

She settled into the couch, then leaned her head back and closed her eyes. Nothing else she could do right now. She had sowed the seed of doubt and had made him worry for his wife and his kids, but, beyond that, she'd have to wait and see. It would be a cat-and-mouse affair. It just remained to be seen who would be the damn mouse.

IT TOOK TWO bullets, one from each gun, to drop the two armed men facing them. Gavin and Shane didn't shoot them to kill, but one had moved into the bullet and had unfortunately died on the spot. The other one, realizing his partner was down, was already holding his shoulder, where the other bullet went, crying like a baby.

Thankfully this tunnel seemed to muffle their shots, as no bad guys came running to check out the noise. And Gavin wasn't too worried about the crying man being heard in either house, as the tunnel was underground, and this odd anteroom seemed to be adjacent the basement to the first house, by his calculation.

Of the third man, there was no sign, though Shane swore he had heard a third voice. Checking to make sure the first man was dead, Shane quickly found a bandanna and some zip ties on the dead man's body. He handed the bandanna and some ties to Gavin, as Shane tied up the injured man's hands behind his back, pushed him into a stray chair in this anteroom, and asked the guy, "Where are they?"

The man just blubbered about his shoulder and needing help.

Shane leaned over and smacked him hard across the face.

"Where'd the third guy go?" But there was no getting any sense out of him. Shane disappeared, on the hunt for the third man, running back toward the second house, since this first house may have even more visitors inside now.

Meanwhile, Gavin kicked away the man's handgun, cocked his own, and held it against the man's head. "Shut the fuck up."

The man took several deep breaths, trying to control his sobbing.

"Where is the old couple?"

His captive's eyes widened, and he shook his head.

"Where are they?"

His eyes darted side to side, but he didn't say anything.

Gavin knocked him off the chair and onto the concrete floor, where he tied up his feet and then tied his bound hands and feet together, behind him, so he couldn't get loose, and stuffed the bandanna in his mouth. Gavin's final act was to pick up the two guns off the floor, stuffing one in the back of his jeans at the waistband, the other in the front of his waistband, then covering both with his shirt. He carried his firearm in his hand. Then Gavin checked out the next door on the opposite side of the anteroom, testing the waters before diving in.

The basement of the first house. Gavin stepped through.

How had they missed this? Turning around, he studied that entranceway. Seemed one of the walls with shelving served double duty as a secret door to this end of the hidden tunnel.

Gavin quickly did a sweep of its basement once more, hopeful, but found nothing. *Why would you have three guards and nothing to guard?*

Shaking his head and wondering where else the old couple could be, he got a weird feeling. He looked out one of the high basement windows, happy to see the driveway leading to this first house was empty. *So our trio of guards parked elsewhere and walked here. Maybe drove the black truck to the second house, parked it in the garage, bringing the parents with them.*

Then Gavin checked for his vehicle, farther down in that copse, and realized something was wrong. The car door was ajar. Swearing under his breath, he made a split-second decision. He tapped his comm, and Shane answered immediately. "There's a problem at the car."

"Go," Shane said. "I'm fine here."

Taking his buddy at his word, Gavin quickly raced back to the basement anteroom and checked the gunman, who was now bleeding at a decent rate but still alive. Gavin shut that door and bolted across the basement to the other side, quietly climbing the steps to the first floor, stopping at the connecting door. He could hear voices inside this house. Sure enough, it was Rosalina.

Swearing softly under his breath, he listened as she tried to convince this guy that men were coming after him and then he would be in trouble.

She obviously wasn't under extreme duress because of the evenness of her voice. But she was also one damn smart cookie and was trying to get into this guy's head. As Gavin overheard that kids and a pregnant wife were involved, he understood that she was trying to get her gunman to see how his actions would impact his family's lives.

Gavin turned the knob and let his breath out ever-so-gently as the door opened just a hair.

The voices immediately rose in volume as the sounds came through the now-open door. He pushed their voices to the side in his mind, thinking back to the layout of this first house, so he could remember exactly where the basement door was and realized it was through the pantry. He slowly opened the door farther and made his way through the pantry to the kitchen and still found no sign of anyone.

Holding his handgun in front of him, he made it through the kitchen to the dining room, following the trail to the voices. He peered around a doorway, and Rosalina sat on a couch with her back to Gavin, a gunman glaring at her. A huge man with dark skin, pointing a handgun at her and telling her to shut up.

Of course he'd be telling her to shut up, as nothing she had to say he would want to hear.

Gavin turned back and took another route, slipping from the dining room into the front hallway and moved his way around to the back, so he could come up on the other side of the living room. Then he saw another vehicle pull up front.

Swearing softly, he backed up and came around to where he had been before. He could take out the one guy, but that would alert the others outside that trouble was within. That he couldn't have. He needed to take this guy out and get her free and clear, but, as Gavin tried to formulate a plan in the dining room, two men walked in the front door.

The dominant one, the obvious leader, strode in with

purpose, the other following him. When the leader took one look at her, he called out, "Great, you got one."

"Yeah," the big man said. "I did. So bonus for me, right?"

"Absolutely," the leader said, and he pulled out his handgun and fired. In a split second, a round hole appeared in the mammoth of a man, and he dropped at Rosalina's feet.

CHAPTER 11

ROSALINA RECOILED IN shock, as the huge man fell to the floor with a hole in his head. She didn't make a sound, but involuntary trembling racked her body with violent shivers. She stared in shock at the two new arrivals. "Why did you do that?" she whispered.

"He wanted a bonus," the leader said carelessly. "So I gave him one."

"He's got two sons, and his wife is pregnant."

"I don't care. He should have thought of that before he got into this business," the leader said. He stood with his hands on his hips and looked at her. "So now what am I supposed to do with you?"

She stared back mutely. She didn't have a clue what had just happened or why. "What is this all about?" she asked. "From the moment we were kidnapped off the street, nobody understood why or what you wanted."

"I don't want anything," he said. "I hired on for the job and hired more contractors to keep myself a little bit removed, but most of the locals are too damn stupid."

"What has this got to do with my parents?" she whispered. She wrapped her arms around her chest, pulling her knees up, so she sat cross-legged, rocking gently on the couch—as if reverting back to a child with the shock of everything that had happened.

"And again I don't really care why," he said in a bold voice. "All I care about is making sure I follow things to the letter, and that means you, I'm afraid, will have to go."

At his words she froze. "*Go?*" she asked faintly. "Please tell me that you're not going to kill me."

"Well, that's what my orders are, yes," he said, "but we need to make it look not quite so violent as this guy."

"I'm supposed to die in an accident, is that the idea?"

"A terrible accident," he said, with a nod. "Isn't that tragic?"

But there was nothing tragic about his tone of voice. There was a detachment to it and almost a hint of amusement as he stared at her.

"Do I at least get to know why or how and who is paying you to do this?" she asked, her fingers tightening into fists as she tried to figure it out. She didn't have a clue who would want her dead. She hadn't thought she had any enemies. But, then again, she hadn't gone out of her way to make any friends either. Were nonfriends then enemies by default? She hoped not because that left seven billion people on the planet who wouldn't mind seeing her dead. What a thought.

"No, that's part of the deal," he snapped. "I'm not allowed to say anything."

"So, do I get to meet this person who's paying you?" she asked, her voice unsteady. "Do I get to meet the person who has ordered my demise?"

He shrugged. "Not exactly sure yet. Now that we have you, I'll check in and see what they want to do."

She kept her thoughts to herself as she heard the word *they*. So multiple people wanted her out of the equation? What had she done to deserve this? "Is same fate planned for my parents too?" she asked. She studied his face, looking for any sign that her parents were alive.

"Maybe," he said. "Remember? I'll check in."

"And so, do you have them too?"

"We never lost them," he said. "Not exactly sure how you two got loose though."

"Is it true that you killed the boss of the guy who tied me up? If so, that is too damn bad because he did a good job of it."

"Not if you got loose," he said. "Incompetence is not allowed."

She had never even considered that her getting loose could have had an impact on another person like that. She didn't even remember much, having come to in the chair, and then very rapidly seeing her sister across the table from her. "What about my sister?"

"What about her?" he snapped carelessly.

"Well, she's loose too."

"I know," he said. "You both escaped."

"So I'm only the one being punished?"

"I didn't say that," he said. "For all you know, we've already gone after her at the hotel again."

"And have you?" she asked.

He just shot her a look and pulled out his phone to make a call. He motioned at the second man as he stepped away. "Keep an eye on her. She's tricky." And he walked out the front door, shutting it forcefully to stand on the veranda. He paced back and forth as he spoke on the phone.

What she wouldn't do to have the ability to hear what he said. This was just too damn unbelievable. And she still had no idea where Gavin and Shane were either. Surely they were close.

She studied the second man, but he had an insolent look on his face as he studied her up and down. One of those creepy looks that said he'd like a few minutes alone with her before her "accident." She pulled her knees up tight against her chest and held herself still.

"You should be scared," he said.

"What's it do for me?" she asked. "Guys like you thrive on fear."

"You don't know anything about me," he said.

"No," she said, with a wave of her hand, "but I know the type. You thrive on making everybody else afraid of you. It's how you operate. With women in particular. You beat them up if they don't do what you want, and you rape them just to prove that you can."

Instantly the smile fell from his face. "You don't know anything about me, bitch." And he stormed toward her.

She glared at him. "Go ahead and mark me up," she said. "You'll have to make sure it's a damn good accident to hide previous injuries."

That stopped him in his tracks. He took a deep breath and let it out slowly. "That'll be enough out of you."

"Or what?" she said in disgust.

"Or I'll get a gag," he said. "And I'll make sure it's damn tight."

"Again, previous injuries," she said. "Do you really think the cops won't figure out I was gagged before you shoved me in a vehicle and tossed me over a cliff?"

"Well, if they already know that," he said, "it won't matter if I blow apart your knees or chop off a finger, will it?"

"You should probably talk to your boss about that first," she said with a sneer. "You're not calling the shots, and neither is he. You're both being paid. You're nothing but little errand boys."

He laughed. "You can't get my goat by insulting me," he said. "I've been called worse."

"By the victims, I'm sure," she said. "I wonder what your mama would think if she knew this is what you did for a living."

"You leave my mama out of this," he roared. "She's in heaven, smiling down on what I'm doing."

"Yeah, was she just like you then?"

"My mama was an angel," he said, his gaze narrowing on her face. "Nobody gets to insult my mama."

"Maybe not," she said, "but imagine how she feels, looking at what you're doing with your life. She couldn't stay and enjoy her life and wanted only the best for you. And look. You're just throwing it all away."

"I'm not throwing nothing away," he said. "I'm making money so I can leave this godforsaken island and go live like a king."

"That'll be fun," she said. "In order to be king, you have to be king over someone. So … what? You'll enslave a dozen people so you're a leader and a boss?"

He pulled back and glared at her. "Just shut up," he said and paced back and forth, his gaze on his partner outside on the veranda.

"You okay with him making plans without you? You already saw what happened to the other guy he hired."

"We've been working together for a long time," he said. "He needs me."

"Guys like that don't need anybody. Especially not long-term."

"You're not turning me against him," he scoffed. "You think I haven't heard it all before?"

"How many people have you killed?" she asked, inviting him to brag. "Probably none. You sure you're not just all talk?"

"I have so," he said. "And they weren't just cheap little bitches like you."

"Oh, so you've killed, and you think you're a big man, huh?" she scoffed. "Probably teenage boys in their sleep, where they couldn't protest, couldn't fight back."

"Like hell," he roared. "I took out two businessmen here just last month."

"Wow, what did they do? Talk down to you, or not give you a job when you asked for it?"

"The competitor wanted them taken out," he said, laughing. "That's what happens when you get too big for your britches and don't listen to other people."

"You mean, they ran their business smarter and wiser, offering better quality at lower prices, and so this competitor didn't like that and wanted them killed?"

"Doesn't matter. It never helps to get on the wrong side."

"No," she said, "it sure never helps to have everybody be assholes and kill you just because you did a good job. That's hardly the reward they thought they would get."

"Well, it's the way life works," he said.

"Not everywhere," she said. "And, in many cases, not at all."

"Whatever," he said.

"Besides, were you the one who pulled the trigger, or was it your boss there?" she asked.

"He's not my boss, I told you. He's my partner."

"Looks like he's the one making the plans and talking to the big bosses," she said. "So I'm not sure what kind of partnership that is."

"You don't know anything," he said, turning around to look at his partner. "And they prefer to deal with him."

"Of course," she said. "He's probably the saner of the two of you. Probably the more businesslike."

"Like hell," he growled. "He just does better bitching with people like that."

"Yeah, you just want to kill them, right?"

"No, not until I take their money," he said, laughing.

"You killed any of the people who hired you?"

"No," he said. "Why would I?"

"Right, there might not be return business, is that it?" she asked.

"Maybe," he said. "You never can tell."

"I'm surprised you're even known to them at all."

"They don't know who we are," he sneered. "You'd never do well in this business."

"Of course not," she said with a heavy sigh. "Why would I? I'm honest, loyal, and up-front. I try to avoid dealing with people who betray me."

"Well, you must have sucked at that too because somebody sure as hell doesn't want you alive."

She thought about that for a long moment, then gave a clipped nod. "You're right. I never spent time currying favor. I figured people would take me as I am and would realize who I was inside."

"It doesn't matter who you are inside," he said. "Either you play the game or you get kicked off the track."

"Interesting game you're playing," she said. "It sucks though. Because you never know when the track changes and when the game becomes something completely different."

"Maybe," he said, "but it sounds to me like you just did

something wrong or wouldn't play the game right, and so they're removing you. That's what this kind of stuff is always about. Either somebody is an obstacle to somebody else's expansive growth or an obstacle to something they want."

"Meaning, I'm an obstacle? As in, I've voted against something or have money that somebody else wants?"

"Something like that," he said. "Often lately it's been obstacles to something somebody wants."

"How does that work?" she asked, genuinely curious now. "Somebody decides somebody's doing better than they are, so they hire you to just take out the opponent?"

"Makes it simpler," he said. "As long as you got the money, you can take out anybody you want."

"*As long as you've got the money,*" she murmured, nodding to herself. "So, it goes without saying that your clients must all be wealthy."

"Of course," he said. "What would be the point of working for somebody who's poor?"

"Well, it depends. Have you got a percentage in there, for increased growth and profits, based on how the situation will look for them after the person they want taken out is gone?"

He looked momentarily confused.

She explained. "Well, you could try fulfilling somebody's request, but, instead of taking a lump sum payment, you get say 10 percent of their profits for the next five years."

He stared at her in surprise with a quick frown. "And who'll make sure that they pay us?" he sneered.

"Well, if you don't get paid, they'll get the same treatment you gave to their victim, right?"

He shrugged, obviously not liking her suggestion.

It made sense to her, but then again she wasn't into this

lovely little business. While they watched and waited, the boss man continued to walk back and forth on the veranda. "Looks like the conversation is getting a bit heated," she said.

"It's serious business," he said. "We need to get an idea of what they want."

"Of course because you've got to deliver it. And, if you don't deliver it right, then there's a lot of danger of getting caught."

"We've never been caught yet," he snapped.

"So the cops don't know anything about you? What about the government guys?"

"The government doesn't know anything," he said. "Black ops? Hah! That just means completely in the dark. And that's all we've ever found. Stupid men who don't know anything."

"I guess you haven't known the right men then, have you?"

"Or," he sneered, "maybe you haven't."

"And maybe the ones you do know have been keeping your path nice and smooth."

"Of course," he said, "that's what we've paid them for."

"So, you pay them enough to keep them off your back?"

"That's how the world works," he said.

"In some places, yes," she admitted sadly. "I guess, in my own way, I've always hoped for a better world out there. Instead it seems like, every time I turn around, I'm caught up with this underbelly that's dark, dank, and ugly."

"Well, I've been brought up in that underbelly," he said. "So, when you know how to navigate through this hell, it's not too bad. And there's a way to make a world of difference in it."

"You mean, a world of difference for yourself," she said,

"because you sure as heck aren't doing anything to help anybody else, are you?"

"No way," he said. "It's every man for himself."

"Exactly," she said. "So, when your boss is done with you," she said, "he'll just knock you off, like he did this guy." She stared down at the man on the floor, shaking her head. "His poor kids. His poor wife."

"Yeah, his wife is a looker too," he said. "I'll have to go pay her a private visit."

Rosalina's blood ran cold at that. "Is that really who you are?"

"Why not?"

Just then the boss finished his phone call and walked toward the front door. Her guard looked at her and grinned. "Now you're in for it."

GAVIN HAD ALREADY checked out the living room and the rest of the lower part of the house as he watched the boss man pace back and forth on the front veranda. He wished he could hear the conversation, but the boss man's voice was too quiet, and too many walls were between them. Gavin tapped his comm, waiting for Shane to answer. Finally Shane responded that he was in position. "Good. Make sure you get this guy and take him out."

"I've got the one outside," Shane confirmed.

"I've got the one inside," Gavin said. He snuck down the hallway and waited for the moment when the guy's back was turned. Out of the corner of his eye, Gavin saw Shane coming up on the side of the boss, as he stood there with his hands on his hips as he thought about his next move. He was staring out across the field, and his partner waited for him to come inside. Gavin needed the inside man to look elsewhere, so Shane could get up behind the leader. Gavin deliberately banged the table beside the front door, just out of sight.

"What the hell?" the gunman roared and came racing toward him.

Gavin stepped around the corner just as the inside man came barreling around with his gun out. As soon as Gavin caught sight of the gun, he grabbed it and the arm holding it and immediately smacked the guy's arm hard against his thigh, breaking his bones with an audible *crunch*, his fist then going next in a hard uppercut to the gunman's jaw. As the guy came to a sudden stop, Gavin took out his knees, dropped him onto the ground, pulled both his hands back behind him, and pinned him in place.

Kicking the handgun away, Gavin turned him, giving another hard fist to the side of his head, knocking him out completely. Turning, Gavin saw Rosalina standing there, a shocked look on her face. "Find something to tie him up with," he said urgently.

She nodded and raced to the kitchen, returning with heavy zip ties.

He loved those things. He quickly laced two together and then tied up the hands and then the ankles of his prisoner. Thereafter he picked him up by the collar and dragged him into the kitchen, where he lay him on the floor and left him there.

"Grab a tea towel or a dishcloth or something and stuff it in his mouth as a gag."

As she raced around the kitchen looking for something, Gavin headed back out in the front yard, finding Shane standing there with no sign of the boss. Gavin raced outside and saw the blood pouring down Shane's leg. "Shit," he said.

"You mean, double shit," Shane said, his tone mild, but he was putting pressure on his thigh.

"How bad is it?"

"Just bad enough to keep me from taking off after him," he said. "I'll go grab something to take care of this." He pointed across the field. "He went in that direction."

With a second look at his friend's face but reassured, Gavin took off across the driveway, past the vehicles, and headed to the field. He could easily see the tracks as the gunman kept running. Gavin ran as fast as he could across the field, looking for the boss man, but Gavin also had to consider the guy ahead of him knew the area and definitely had a gun. Just then a shot whizzed past his head, lifting the hair beside his ear. He hit the ground and then reassessed.

Trees were off to the side, but he, of course, was following the tracks cutting the cleanest path. He immediately changed direction and ran in a zigzag pattern to the trees. Two more shots came his way. Even as they came, he couldn't see the shooter because the gunman crouched in the tall grass.

Gavin wove his way through the brush and the trees, heading up until he thought he was closer to the gunman. One nearby tree was a little taller, so he quickly grabbed a lower limb and swung himself up to get a better idea.

As he looked out through the branches, he saw his quarry, sitting in the long grass, looking for him. Gavin immediately pulled out his handgun, lined up a shot, and fired. The gunman hopped up with a roar, limping, and started to run out of gun range. Gavin couldn't let that happen, so he lined up a second shot and took out the other leg.

Down he went.

But now Gavin had an injured man who was down but still armed. Gavin couldn't line up a shot to take out the gun due to the long grass, which is what Gavin should have done next. So he dropped to the ground and quickly raced toward the gunman, calling out, "Stay down and keep that goddamn gun down."

"Fuck you," the gunman said and started shooting.

"You do that," he said, "and all you'll do is run out of bullets."

Immediately he stopped.

"I'm coming," Gavin said, "and, if you fire once more, I promise there'll be a bullet in the center of your forehead, just like you gave that other guy."

And there was, indeed, one more shot. But it didn't come Gavin's way. Swearing softly, he raced forward and finally came upon the gunman, his hand up against his head, and the gun flat against his skull. The other side of his head had been blown apart. He'd taken the last bullet and had put it into his own brain.

Gavin stood here, swearing still, as he pulled out his phone and quickly called his team. "This gunman took his own life," he said. "Goddammit."

"What about the other one?" Lennox asked.

"He's tied up in the kitchen with Rosalina. Shane took a bullet in the leg. We need a team here with forensics and medics fast."

"They're already on the way," Lennox said. "Just hang tight."

"I'm going back," he said, "to make sure Shane is okay." Stopping, he reached down and pulled out the gunman's wallet. "First I'm sending you photos of this guy and his

ID." He laid all the cards on the man's chest and took photographs and quickly sent them to Lennox. "See if you can do something with that. From what I overheard, he was hired for the job, and they were supposed to make Rosalina's death look like an ugly accident, maybe her parents as well."

"So all three of them were supposed to die?" Lennox's voice was sharp. "What about the other sister?"

"Rosalina mentioned it when she was talking to the guy, but he didn't confirm or deny that she was supposed to be killed in the same way—or killed at all for that matter. It's hard to know. What I did catch," he said, "when I was listening to him talk to Rosalina, was how once he used the pronoun *they*. As in the lead gunman would call, and *they* will make a decision."

"So, more than one mastermind?"

"That was my take on it too." He quickly put everything back into the guy's wallet and then put it in his pocket. Gavin checked him for anything else and pulled out a set of car keys and a cell phone. "His vehicle is here too," he said. He pressed the key fob button and heard a resounding beep from a vehicle parked in front of the first house. "I'll take a quick look at that."

"Forensics will be about twenty minutes," Lennox said.

"Good. I've got to check the vehicle and then Shane. This guy, well, I've already done a full search on him. So, unless there's something I missed, he won't be a whole lot of use. But run his prints and names and see if we can confirm his ID, get some of his family and friends ID'd too. There's got to be a connection somewhere. Somebody is after Rosalina and her parents, and just because this guy is done and gone doesn't mean Rosalina's out of danger."

"And we still have to find the parents."

"Yes," he said. "And that won't be the easiest thing either. Also we've got the three men from the tunnel. Two are dead. By now Shane should have sent you their photos and any IDs off their persons. I suspect they all drove in with the black truck and the old couple, but hopefully forensics can match their prints to the vehicle and/or to any other crimes."

"We'll keep you posted," Lennox said and rang off.

Knowing time on his own to search was limited, Gavin raced to the gunman's vehicle in front of the first house and checked the driver's side. Nothing helpful was inside the vehicle that he could see. He went over to the passenger side, pulled out the insurance papers, and, though it was under a different name than the dead guy's IDs, Gavin quickly took images of everything he found and sent it to Lennox too.

He found a scrap of notepaper with just a cell phone number on it. He took a photo of that and sent it off to Lennox as well. The fact that it was handwritten could mean something. Chances were good it would also mean nothing. Hopefully it would and could add a nail to one of these assholes' coffins, … all the better. He quickly checked the back seat and just found fast-food wrappers and a couple juice jugs.

He opened up the trunk, and that was a bit more interesting, as he found rope, gloves, cotton bandannas, and a couple sets of handcuffs. He took photos of it all, sending them off to Lennox. Once he sent photos of the license plates and a couple of the vehicle itself, he closed up the car and raced into the house. There he found Rosalina in the kitchen, looking after Shane, who smiled cheerfully and said, "Just a flesh wound."

"It's hardly a flesh wound," Rosalina said crossly. "You could have been badly injured." And, indeed, she must have cut open Shane's jeans to clean the wound and now pressed a bandage against the wound. She was in the process of tying it securely in place. She looked at Gavin. "How did you fare?"

"My guy turned the gun on himself," he said soberly. "Found his vehicle and I've got a pile of fake names and fake documents for my team to go through, but I didn't take any more time up there." He also held up the jotted-down phone number. "Do you know what that number is?"

She shook her head. "No. Where did you find it?"

"On the floor in the passenger seat of the gunman's car."

She frowned. "I don't think it's a local number, is it?"

"No, I don't think so," he said. "I have half a mind to dial it, but I don't want anybody to know I've got it, should it be connected to the person behind all this." He walked over to the man he had on the floor and rolled him over to see hot dark eyes glaring at him. "And this, of course, is our talker."

Only the man couldn't speak because of the gag. Gavin pulled out the gag, lifted his prisoner up, and sat him on a chair with his arms uncomfortably behind him, so he had to sit at the edge. "So, this is your one chance to talk," he said.

"Fuck you," the guy said.

"Well, your buddy is dead, so your connection to whoever was paying you for this is gone. So, now you aren't getting any money, and you've already admitted to Rosalina that you shot and killed two businessmen a month ago," Gavin said cheerfully. "You'll be in jail for a hell of a long time, so you might as well fess up and make it easy on yourself."

"You'll get yours," he said.

"Well, it won't be at your hand," Gavin said with a smile.

He shrugged. "Nobody said just the two of us were working on this job." He sneered at Rosalina and the two guys. "Like I said, you'll get yours."

CHAPTER 12

ROSALINA LOOKED AT Gavin, chewing on her bottom lip.

He shrugged. "Don't worry about it. We've kept you safe so far."

She nodded. "But this time, one of you got shot."

"It's just a flesh wound," Shane protested. "That hardly counts, and no way you're taking me out of the game at this point in time."

"If you can't walk, you're out of the game," Gavin said. "And, if you're leaving a blood trail, you're out of the game."

Shane glared at him. "I'll be fine, and you damn well know it."

And Gavin knew Shane would be because that's the kind of man he was. Gavin looked down at his uncooperative prisoner and told him to stand up. The guy just ignored him. Gavin tapped him hard against the jaw, rendering him unconscious, then rolled him back to the ground, where he checked his wallet and his pockets. He put the contents of his pockets onto the table and then opened the guy's wallet. A decent amount of cash was in the back and a bunch of IDs. Gavin quickly laid them all out on the table and took photographs of them.

"What's the rush?" she asked, as she studied the pictures. "And who knew his name was Polly?"

"Yeah, the other guy, his name was Marka," he said. "I don't know if those are real names are not. We've got addresses here too."

"Interesting, right?"

"Somebody needs to tell the third guy's wife that he's not coming home," she said, with a glance toward the living room, where the mammoth male lay dead.

"The cops will handle that," he said.

She sighed. "Two dead already."

"Three. Maybe a fourth in the tunnel that connects these two houses. At least that's all we know of here alone," he said. "Don't forget the warehouse."

She winced at that. "Will Polly be just as uncooperative as that sniper guy?"

"Probably," he said. "What we still don't know is who's behind all this."

"Exactly," she said. "And how does Polly have so much money?" She rifled through the money, which was mostly in larger denominations.

"He's probably been prepaid for a certain amount of the job," Gavin said. "He'd get the rest when he was done."

"Scary thought," she said. "Somebody's life reduced to just these bills."

"Not just somebody's life," he said. "Your life."

She frowned. "That makes it even worse."

"Exactly." Gavin nodded. "The local law enforcement are on their way," Gavin said, "and they won't be happy."

"Maybe not," she said indignantly, "but we had to rescue ourselves."

He chuckled as she stood up, walked closer. He wrapped his arms around her and held her close. He knew it was more shock than anything, but she was the sweetest thing to hug him. And he knew that she'd shoot him for even thinking it. "It's okay now," he whispered. "We got the kidnappers."

"I know," she said, her voice muffled against her shirt. "But," she murmured, "the masterminds behind it are still unknown and on the loose."

"Right," he said. "Give us an hour here, and then we'll get you back to the hotel."

"That would be nice," she said, yawning. "I still need sleep."

"Lucky you. At least you got some," he said with a grin. In the distance, he heard sirens coming. "Here's the cavalry. Where's your phone?

"I need to get it back from the big guy," she said.

"Good. Let's get this all over with."

More than an hour later they finally managed to leave, and it was two hours before they got to the hotel. Grateful they could go straight up to her room, she walked in and looked at the bed, exhausted. "Is Shane coming up?"

"He's getting stitches. We'll pick him up in about six hours," he said. "Get some sleep while you can."

"You're the one who's probably about to drop."

He nodded, pulled his shirt over his head, kicked off his shoes, and then off came his socks. Unzipping his jeans, he stepped out of them, leaving him in his boxers. Completely natural and unaffected by her stare, he walked to the bed, pulled the blankets back so they were almost off, then pulled the sheet back and crawled under, pulling the sheet up on top of him.

"Just like that?" she asked, amused.

He gave her a glance. "Unless you're crawling in here with me," he said, "yes."

"And if I do crawl in there with you?" she asked with

interest.

"You'll have to wait till I wake up," he said, "because I need to recharge." And, even as she watched, he slowly dropped into a deep sleep.

She didn't think she'd seen anything like it before. She, on the other hand, although tired, wasn't sure she'd drop off half as fast. She stepped out of her clothes, went to the bathroom, and scrubbed her face and her hands before coming back, dressed in only a T-shirt and panties. She stared from one bed to the other, then realized she didn't want to sleep alone.

There was no way to push the two beds together with the night tables in between them, so she walked over to his bed and slipped under the covers on the empty side. She wondered if this kidnapping event would impact her long-term or not. She wasn't used to being susceptible to fears of boogeymen in the dark. She had always been so very clear-cut about her choices in life, and this was no different. She didn't want to be alone right now. And he was a hell of a good choice as a teddy bear.

As she dozed in and out, never really getting into a deep sleep, she felt him rolling over, and finally he wrapped his arms around her, pulled her back against his chest, and whispered, "Sleep. You really need it."

And she dropped off. When the furnace that was wrapped all around her woke her back up again, she thought she had slept only for like twenty minutes. They remained in their initial position, with his chest to her back. The sheet was off, and his hands were stroking her, exploring and finding all the curves and crevices of her body, like she'd never been explored before. Not only was it a sensuous experience but it was intriguing.

As he found a little nook and explored it, she could almost sense his mind wondering about where and what because, of course, he still lay behind her. She didn't know how, but his fingers were doing the seeing for him. It was intense, as overwhelming nerve sensations covered her body as his hands drifted up her calves and her knees, checking out the little bumps on her kneecap to slide behind it.

That almost made her laugh out loud, and she didn't realize how ticklish she was. Well, when his hand slipped across the part of her lower belly into her panties and the curls at the apex of her thighs and then down, she cried out and shifted against him. He slid down ever-so-slightly, the ridge inside his boxers positioned tight against her cheeks, and his fingers got busy between her legs. She reached down to push away his hand, but he wasn't having anything to do with it.

She cast about as he found the tiny nub on her body, already responding as she tried to evade the teasing stroke of those devilish fingers. But every movement she made rubbed her buttocks against the hard ridge behind her. It was a double erotic sensation from both front and back, and her body was quickly turning into jelly.

Just when she thought she couldn't stand it anymore, she was flipped onto her back, stripping away her T-shirt at the same time. He was suddenly over her and between her thighs, his body hot and heavy right above her. She looped her arms around his neck and tugged him down. "Good morning," she whispered, before their lips touched.

He slowly lowered some of his weight on top of her, his tongue busy as he stroked and caressed her lips before plunging deep into her mouth. When he lifted his head, he whispered, "Good morning."

"Is this usually the way you wake up?"

He nodded, a slight chuckle escaping. "When I find a beautiful woman in my bed, I do."

"Ah, so that's what the trick is," she said, lifting her chest ever-so-slightly, the gentle arch brushing her breasts against his hot chest.

"Well, when the invitation is there," he whispered, sliding his tongue in and out of her mouth, gently warring with her tongue.

She smiled and tightened her arms around his neck, pulling him closer. "Definitely an invitation," she murmured.

And he kissed her while the passion rose quickly between them. He slid his hands down and underneath her to pull down her panties.

Smiling, she said, "We're still wearing too many clothes, aren't we?"

"We are," he said.

She slid her hands down to cup his heavily muscled cheeks, sliding under the boxers to tuck them farther down. And, when she couldn't get them to go any farther because they were out of reach, she slid a hand down to the front of his hips, gently grasping him with her hand.

He sucked in his breath, his hips coming forward to give her better access.

She gently stroked the full length of him, only to cup him down below and then slide back up again. With the soft material of his boxers pulled back, she rolled over to the side. She quickly slipped both hands down to his hips and pulled off the material. He rolled onto his back, now fully exposed and completely comfortable.

She stared at his heavily muscled chest, his massive biceps, and taut belly and whispered, "You'd make a great model."

He chuckled. "I have no interest in inviting anybody to stare at me," he said.

She pulled the boxers all the way off his legs, loving his heavy quads and seeing the various little bits and pieces of scars and damage. His massive feet compared to her own made her stop and pause. She quickly stood, tossing off her panties, then walked to the end of the bed. She lifted one of her feet to rest against his own and said, "Your feet are literally twice as big as mine."

He sat up and took a look, then whispered, "Obviously I need to have them that size."

She crawled up beside him, completely amazed. "I just can't imagine so much strength," she said, "so much virility."

His hands were gentle as they stroked down her sides to her hips, sliding back up to cup her breasts. "So much femininity," he whispered. "So delicate, so beautiful, so soft, and yet so damn strong inside." And he tugged her back down to the bed beside him.

She smiled, opened her arms, and pulled him over her. "Strong inside, yes," she said, "and I guess the way of the world is for women to have that strength and yet to still show the softness on the outside. A complete reversal from men, who show only strength on the outside and yet have that softness within."

He leaned down and kissed her gently. His fingers once again stroking up and down her body, bringing them back to that same fevered pitch, as he whispered, "That's why we're a perfect fit. Male to female, yang to yin, strength to hardness." He spoke as he slid just inside the entrance to her body.

Smiling, she shifted gently. "The good thing is, I won't break," she said, "so come on in." He slid ever-so-gently, not sure that he could take her at her word, but her muscles and tissues softened and warmed, making a space for him inside. When he was finally seated all the way home, she reached up, cupped his face, and said, "Perfect fit."

He nodded. "I didn't think it'd be quite so easy," he whispered.

"Well, it was. Because that was meant to be." And she slowly rocked her hips side to side, shuffling, trying to get him to move.

He smiled down at her. "And just what do you want?" he asked, in a teasing voice.

She smiled up at him. "I want everything you've got to give."

He ground his hips deep against her and started to move. And the pace he set was hard and fast, at a tempo she didn't think she could sustain. Her body rose into a crescendo of emotions and feelings as her nerve endings came to the edge of the world and exploded, sending pulsating waves through her body. When she heard him explode above and beyond, just feeling his eruption deep inside sent more shock waves through her body, until she lay here completely trembling in shock.

He shifted his weight, pulling over to her side, and tucked her up close. "You okay?"

With the shivers still racking her body, she whispered, "I will be. But wow."

He kissed her gently and tenderly, their fever rising instantly.

"Surely not so soon again?" But she could feel him and the hard ridge already firming up against her belly.

"It's you," he said. "Just something about you."

"How about us?" she whispered, her thighs widening and welcoming him back into the heart of her.

"I'm good either way," he said. And just when she thought that he would set the same crazy tempo, instead he slowed down to painstakingly slow movements, as skin rubbed against skin and muscles held, then lost their grip as movements slid back and forth. It was exquisitely tender and as deliciously sweet as the second climax swirled through them both.

When he collapsed beside her the second time, she murmured, "That was the nicest thing I've ever felt in my life."

"Well, we can repeat it later," he promised.

"I hope so," she whispered. "That and so much more."

"You're so different right now," he murmured, his nose gently rubbing against hers.

"No," she said. "Not really. I just let down my guard a bit. I'm starting to realize I've never really let it down before."

"I don't want to hurt you," he said.

She smiled. "Were you planning on it?"

He looked at her in surprise. "No, of course not," he said.

"Is this just for tonight?" she asked. She didn't want a one-night stand, and yet she didn't want to withdraw from him in bed, but she'd known that was a possibility going into this.

"Not on my part," he said, trailing kisses down her cheek. "I'm definitely looking for longer term than that."

"Well, let's just keep it wide open and see what we've got. I've always been practical, analytical," she said, "but, right now, I just want to let the emotions and the feelings soar through me. It's such a unique experience."

"And you look beautiful in it," he said, in all seriousness. He kissed her again. "Before we head back into a third mind-drugging hot and sweaty sex session, we need to check the time." Just then his phone rang. He leaned across her to grab his phone off the night table and checked the Caller ID. "Shane, how are you doing?"

"I'm fine," he said. "Just waiting for a pickup, unless you want me to take a cab."

"No," he said. "I'll come get you."

"Well, if you get waylaid, and you're not here in fifteen, I'll grab a cab anyway."

"Gotcha." He tossed the phone back down on the night table, kissed her hard, and said, "Hold that thought." Then he got up and redressed.

She sat up in the bed, the sheet pulled around her waist. "Any chance I can stay here?"

He considered it and said, "I'm not really a fan of that idea."

"But the door will be locked," she said in a reasonable tone. "I just want to sleep a bit more if I can."

"We'll be back in thirty at the most," he said.

"Right," she said. "Your choice. I guess I can come." With that, she hopped up to get dressed. She looked at him and said, "Although it would be much nicer to stay in bed with you."

He laughed. "I agree," he said, "but we can't do that right now."

"Right." Dressed, the two of them headed to the door. He reached for her hand as they headed to the elevator.

"So much has happened," she murmured.

"It has, indeed." The elevator was upstairs two floors.

"I should answer my sister. She texted me earlier," she said, stifling a yawn.

"Yeah, we should," he said, but he didn't sound too convinced.

She looked over at him. "What do you know that I don't know?"

He smiled. "Not a whole lot. I'm more concerned about your parents."

"I know," she said, her tone subdued. "Did we ever get an update from the forensic people at the country house? Any chance my parents were there?"

He pulled out his phone as they waited for the elevator. He sent a message to Lennox. **I'm up. What's new? Any sign of the parents?**

Parents have been found.

"Holy shit," he said. "Your parents were found in a hidden shed in the back of the second property."

GAVIN STARED AT that information, surprised.

"Well, that's good news," she said. "Now I feel like we should have stayed and searched for them."

"Well, thankfully the cops did a full search on both properties."

"I'm so glad to hear that. Can we go see them at the hospital then?" Suddenly she stopped and looked up at him. "Are they alive?" she asked, her voice dropping to the barest whisper.

He was already texting Lennox. When he saw the answer, he nodded. "Yeah, they both are."

"Oh, thank God."

He said, "We'll find them at the hospital when we get there."

She squeezed his fingers hard. "Do you suppose anyone told my sister?"

He frowned. "I don't know," he said. "Do you want to make a quick detour and tell her?"

She nodded. "It's the right thing to do."

When they got into the elevator, it was set to go all the way down. He canceled the request and chose Melinda's floor. As it opened two floors above, they got out and walked to the door. He knocked and noticed that Rosalina was still hanging onto his hand. He was surprised that she was okay with being demonstrative because she didn't seem to be the type, but then a lot had changed in her world.

When nobody answered the door, he looked at her.

She frowned and said, "It's possible they're still asleep. Although she was texting me earlier, wanting to meet for breakfast."

"It is possible." He thought he heard something, then put his ear against the door and knocked again. He frowned, pulled a tool out of his back pocket, and quickly unlocked the door, stepping inside. As they walked in, he called out, "Anybody here?"

He closed the door and, pulling her behind him, went and searched the suite from the bathroom, around to where the bedroom was. And there, on the bed, was Melinda, tied up and gagged.

CHAPTER 13

ROSALINA RACED TO her sister's side and quickly removed the gag. Her sister bawled on the bed. Gavin undid her ties and asked her, "Who did this?"

She shook her head. "A man came in wearing a mask, and, before I knew it," she said, "I was tied up here."

"Where are the kids and Steve?" Rosalina asked.

"He took them to the pool," she said, sitting up and rubbing at her wrists. "I was supposed to join them, and this man came in as I opened the door."

"Do you know who it was?"

"No," she said, tears in her eyes. "God, why is this happening?" She turned to look at the two of them. "Why are you here?"

"They found Mom and Dad," Rosalina said. "We're going to the hospital to see them."

Immediately Melinda hopped to her feet and said, "I'm coming."

"Wait. We need to have the cops come and deal with your room and you," Gavin said. "One thing at a time," and he was already on the phone.

She glared at him. "I don't want to talk to the cops," she said.

"What?" Rosalina stared at her sister in shock. "You were just attacked in your own room. What if it was your kids next time?"

Melinda just glared at her.

"I don't understand," Rosalina said.

"Forget about it," Melinda said. "That's not important. Let's go to the hospital and see Mom and Dad." And she raced out, grabbing her purse as she went.

Feeling something was incredibly off, Rosalina followed as Gavin closed and locked the door behind them. She looked up at him. "What's going on?"

"You tell me," he said. "She's your sister."

She rolled her eyes at that. "I don't understand this person at all," she said. "This is beyond belief."

"Well," he said, "something is happening." As they went to the elevator, it closed right in front of them, with her sister inside, staring out at them.

"Did she really just do that?" Rosalina cried out.

"Is there a reason why she wants to get to your parents before you do?" Gavin asked, suddenly turning to look at her.

She stared at him in horror and said, "I hope not."

"Let's go find out."

"We need to get there faster if we can."

He said, "Let's take the stairs." He bolted down the stairs, but he had the phone against his ear already. She couldn't even hear the conversation as they ended up in the parking garage, and, when they raced out to the front, a vehicle pulled up to them, and they hopped in. "How's your sister getting there?"

Rosalina looked at him in shock. "I don't know," she said. "Maybe a taxi, the same as us?"

They ended up outside the hospital a few minutes later. He was up and out of the car, his hand out, reaching for her.

GAVIN

She immediately put her hand in his, feeling the extra power of his intent as they raced forward.

Inside, he asked where the married couple was and what their current condition was. They were in the emergency room and both still unconscious, according to the nurse. As they walked into the emergency area, several men stepped in front of them. Gavin eyed them carefully and said, "You better let me inside."

Both men shook their heads.

Gavin smiled and said, "You've got three chances."

The men looked at him, and one said, "We have our orders."

"You might have orders," Rosalina said, "but those are my parents."

They looked at her, shrugged, and said, "Nobody's allowed in."

"According to whom?" she asked. But they didn't answer. She looked over at Gavin and saw the tick flickering on the side of his face and knew that something would happen. She darted to the left, but the man standing in front of her blocked her. She called out to the doctor behind him.

The doctor looked at her, frowning, and asked, "Who are you?"

"My parents are here," she said. "We were all kidnapped together. I need to see them!"

He frowned, looked at the two men, and said, "I don't know what's going on," he said, "but this is a hospital."

"It is," Gavin said. He stepped forward and did something, and the first man went down without a sound. Gavin looked at the second man and said, "Your choice."

He looked at the man on the ground and frowned. "What did you do to him?"

"Who said I did anything?" Gavin asked, with the most innocent of looks. "Let's get real. It's a hospital. He's here getting treatment."

The man stared at him suspiciously and said, "I'm under orders that nobody is allowed to come through."

"If you don't tell me who those orders are from," he said, "we'll have a bigger problem than you can imagine."

"Your threats don't upset me," he sneered.

"Good, because, at this point in time," he said, "there's still a shit ton to find out." He pulled out an ID and flashed it in front of him.

The guy frowned and said, "I still don't know if you're allowed through here, sir."

But, as he turned, Rosalina had already raced forward. She disappeared behind the white curtain. Gavin looked at him and said, "Remember that woman. She's the daughter. Nobody else gets in here. Not even the other daughter. She's my number one suspect."

Just then the other man on the floor groaned. Gavin helped him to his feet and said, "You okay, bud?"

The guy gave a hard shake of his head, looked at his partner, and asked, "What happened?"

The guy just looked at him. "I don't have a clue. You were standing there, and, the next thing I know, you're on the ground."

They both looked suspiciously at Gavin, but he just gave them that same blank stare. Rosalina was at the curtain now, and she smiled. "Gavin, come here."

SHE WAITED FOR him to join her at the edge of the curtain.

Both of her parents were here, still unconscious, and the doctors and nurses were working on both. She wrapped her arms around her chest and chewed on the end of her thumbnail.

"Take it easy," he whispered. "At least we have them."

"But why were they even there at that shed in the country? And what the hell was this all about?" she muttered.

He said, "Let's step inside behind the curtain, so nobody can see you. That way, when your sister comes, we'll see what her reaction is."

She nodded.

The doctor looked up and said, "Only her."

Gavin nodded and said, "No problem," and he stepped off to the side. It wasn't very long before Melinda came flying through. She looked at the two guards. Rosalina could hear her sister's voice at the entrance to the emergency room.

"Who are you guarding, and why are you trying to stop me from entering?" she snapped.

The men spoke to her quietly. Melinda's voice was so low that Rosalina couldn't hear. She stared at her parents in shock, realizing just how old and frail they both looked. She missed part of the conversation with Melinda because the doctor spoke to her. She shook her head. "I'm sorry. What did you say?"

"I said that we've got a way to go, but I think they'll be fine," he said. "But they have suffered. They're very dehydrated, and they're both in shock. We'll keep them calm and quiet in a lightly drugged state, while we get their fluids up and do a full assessment. We're sending them for MRIs and X-rays now."

"Oh my," she said, as she studied their bodies. "Are you expecting broken bones?"

"There are signs that they endured some level of violence. Clearly they were roughed up a bit," he said, his tone low. "We just want to make sure we don't have broken bones or internal bleeding."

"Absolutely," she said. "I'm so grateful we found them."

"And just in time too. Now, I understand you're one of two daughters, and you're both here in Honolulu," he said, "so, if your sister is coming, I need you both to avoid disturbing them. We'll move them out of here one at a time, while we run them through a bunch of tests," he explained. "Then we'll set them up in a room together, until we know more."

"Okay, but my sister is not allowed to see them," she whispered. She looked over at her parents. "May I go with them and talk to them?"

"You aren't allowed in the testing areas. However, you can sit with them here, but please don't disturb them. You can gently touch their fingers, but, considering their hands are swollen, maybe don't even do that."

She walked in between the two beds and stared down at her parents. Her hand was at her mouth, tears filling her eyes as she stared at these two who had been the rocks of her world. Not the warm and loving parents of her dreams, but they were her foundation nonetheless. She leaned over and ever-so-gently kissed her father on the cheek.

She whispered, "Dad, you're safe now. We'll get you the help you need." And she went over to her mom and did the same thing. As she straightened, she turned to see two orderlies coming for her father. She sniffled once as they rolled him away. When she looked up, Gavin stood there with a look of compassion on his face.

She walked over and said, shakily, "So it looks like

they'll be okay. They are keeping them sedated a bit, while they get their vitals stabilized. But they'll also run tests to check for broken bones and internal bleeding. Because he thinks they were b-b-beaten." She looked up at him in horror. "Why would anybody beat old people?"

He reached out, and she stepped into his arms and held on tight. "I don't understand," she said, her tears flowing. He gently held her in his arms, his hand stroking her hair and letting her cry. Finally the tears dried up, and she looked up at him. "I don't know if you're good for me or not," she whispered. "I don't normally cry."

"I understand," he said. "But sometimes we all need the release."

She wiped her eyes on her sleeve like a child. And then sighed. "When they are through with Dad, they'll run my mom through the same tests and, at some point, move them to a room."

"Good," he said. "We can't make any decisions until we know exactly what damage was done."

"Their faces are bruised. Somebody actually hit my mom," she whispered. "She's a grandma. Why would you hurt a little old gray-haired lady?" she asked, hating to think of all the fear her mother must have experienced. "I'm just so damn grateful they're here now."

His arms tightened around her, holding her safe.

"That could have been me there too, couldn't it?"

"Yes," he said, "or worse. It definitely could have been, but you're the one who got away."

She smiled at that. "I guess that's a good thing in this instance."

His arms tightened on her note of laughter. He bent down and whispered, "From them, not from me. Got it?"

She looked up at him and smiled. "I'm not interested in getting away from you," she said.

They stood like that for several long moments, and then he whispered, "What do you want to do while we wait?"

"Well, I can sit here until they get the test results. And my sister arrived. Any sign of her?"

At that, they heard Melinda's voice at the ER entranceway, demanding, "Did you let anybody in here?"

One of the men answered her, and she gave a half scream of outrage and came bolting toward them. She glared at her sister, only Gavin keeping her out of her parents' cubicle.

"You said they were here at the hospital. You didn't tell me that you would leave me at the hotel so you could get here first."

Rosalina studied her sister with a totally different perspective. "You didn't tell us why you would bolt past us and slam the elevator doors in our face so you could get here ahead of us," she said coolly. "So, what was so important that you had to get here before I did?"

Melinda glared at her. "It's none of your business," she said.

But that wasn't good enough for Rosalina. "It is my business," she said. "Why did you need to get here first?"

Her sister crossed her arms over her chest, widened her stance combatively, and said, "I wanted to be the one they saw first."

"What difference does it make?" Rosalina asked. "You know you're the one they'll look for first anyway."

"Of course they will. It's not like they want to see you," she sneered.

"I don't understand why you've always hated me," she said. "Obviously I was a younger sibling who you didn't want, but your emotions run awfully deep."

"You were the interloper," Melinda said. "The perfect bloody replacement."

Rosalina stared in shock. "What are you talking about?" she asked. "You were the perfect little girl they always wanted, so they didn't have any time or energy to waste on me."

"Well, I tried not to let them have any," she said, "because I knew that, as soon as they locked onto you and realized just how absolutely perfect in form and brain you were, they wouldn't have any time for me."

Rosalina continued to stare as she tried to figure out what her sister was talking about. "Are you telling me that all those times that you demanded their attention was specifically to ensure they didn't turn their attention to me?"

"Of course," she said. "What other reason would there be?"

"I don't know," she said. "I never did understand that mentality."

"What? There's something you don't know? That's a first."

Rosalina wasn't sure what to do with all the anger and hate coming in her direction. "Seriously? You've hated me all this time for that?"

"Why not?" she said. "I'm the one who had to deal with a missing leg. I'm the one who had to deal with always being not perfect."

"Maybe," she said, "but you also had all of their time, money, and resources that you could ever want. And you got it, so I don't understand why you're concerned now." She thought about all the pain and insecurity and the hours Rosalina had spent crying because she had felt so unloved.

"Did you really feel so inadequate that you had to go out of your way to make my life miserable too?"

Melinda shrugged. "Well, if the choice was you or me, I'd much rather it was you."

That caused Rosalina to burst out laughing. "Well, isn't that the truth?" she said, and her sister grinned at her.

"And did you never wonder about how we looked so different?"

Rosalina's eyebrows shot up. "No," she said. "I never did. Why?"

"Because we don't have the same father," she said. "I'm actually their child. But you are the result of Mom's infidelity."

That blow to her gut hurt so much that she didn't know if it would ever quit. She could feel Gavin holding her tight. In a cool calm voice, he asked, "Do you have proof of that?"

"I don't, but Mom does," she said, with a wave of her hand. "Everybody knew back then."

"I highly doubt Mom would have done something like that," Rosalina said.

Melinda sneered, "Well, she had her days. Don't worry. Mom and Dad were having a lot of trouble, and she decided to go out and live a little. You were the result of that."

"Dad never let on in any way," she said, when she could finally talk. She studied her sister dispassionately, trying to hold the devastating sense of grief inside her at bay. "And, if he isn't my father, who is?"

"Well, that's the question, isn't it?" she said with a smile.

"No," Gavin said. "No more games. Who is her father?"

Instantly Melinda dropped the sneer and glared at him. "What's it to you?" Then she glanced at the close way the two of them were standing, and she rolled her eyes. "Like mother, like daughter apparently."

Rosalina stiffened. "What are you talking about?"

"I'm talking about you and your obvious hookup here," she said with a laugh. "After your failed marriage, all you can do is pick up guys."

"Hardly," Rosalina said. She'd had a lifetime of listening to this crap from her sister. "But did you ever think that maybe it's got something to do with what's going on right now?"

Melinda stared at her in shock. "What are you talking about?"

Gavin immediately spoke up. "Well, both your parents and the two of you were kidnapped," he said, "so maybe Rosalina's birth father had something to do with it?"

"I doubt it," she said. "Besides, I don't think anybody knows." She raised and lowered her eyebrow several times. "If you know what I mean."

"I know what you mean," Rosalina said, her arms across her chest, still trying to hold in the ache. Her mind filled with a million questions. "It still doesn't answer the question, and I don't believe Mom would have gone out with a bunch of random men."

"Well, five minutes ago," her sister said carelessly, "you didn't think she'd have gone with anyone."

"True." And that was still something she struggled with.

Just then the orderly brought her father back. Rosalina stared, devastated to see him lying there in that condition. She looked at the doctor, and he mouthed *X-rays*.

"So, that was why Mom always doted on you?" Rosalina asked, hating the fact that she still needed answers.

"Well, of course she doted on me," Melinda said. "She had to make it up to me, didn't she?"

"Wow," Gavin said. "What an interesting way to look at life. As if they owed you."

"They owed me all right," she said. "You're damn right they owed me. It was supposed to be just me, and I wouldn't have to share my parents with anybody. I shouldn't have had to split the company with anyone. But, no, Mom had to go and have another daughter."

"And what difference does it make?" Rosalina asked.

"Remember how you were so close with Grandpa?"

"Yes," she said, "with Grandma and Grandpa."

"Well, that's because Grandpa was your father," Melinda said, and then she laughed.

Gavin's arms tightened around Rosalina, as if trying to protect her from the blow. "Seriously?" she asked faintly.

Melinda laughed and laughed. "Absolutely. She had an affair with Dad's own father. So, you are actually Dad's half sister."

Rosalina stared at Melinda, who obviously got so much enjoyment and delight when hurting and humiliating Rosalina.

Gavin whispered in her ear, "It's not your fault or your problem, Rosalina. Whatever happened thirty years ago happened for a reason, and the fact is, you're alive today, and that is something wonderful, not something to be ashamed of. You are a perfectly brilliant and beautiful woman, and, no matter how much Melinda's trying to hurt you, don't you let her." As he gently stroked her arm, she twisted ever-so-slightly to stare up at him.

"You are a gift, you know?" she whispered. He stared at her in shock as she smiled. "A lot of people would have fled this room, not wanting anything to do with this ugly sordid mess."

Melinda grunted in disgust, but Gavin and Rosalina ignored her, engrossed in their own conversation, yet still blocking Melinda from access to her parents.

"It takes more than hearing about family garbage to chase me away," he said. "Besides, this isn't on you. This has nothing to do with you. If anything, it makes you all the more amazing to me."

"But then my birth father obviously has nothing to do with what's happening here and now either, does he?"

"Not likely, if it was your grandfather, as both he and your grandmother are deceased. Isn't that correct?"

She nodded slowly. "Yes, my grandfather had a heart attack a few years back, and I can't remember what happened with my grandmother."

"But they looked after you a lot?"

"Yes," Rosalina said, "they did, and I loved them both very dearly."

Melinda cleared her throat, or growled, but was ignored all the same.

"Do you think they knew?" he asked Rosalina.

She shook her head. "How could I ever know?" she asked brokenly. "Maybe? My grandmother sure didn't act like anything was wrong. But I was just a kid, so how would I know? It's not like I had much to compare it to," she said. "I really don't know."

"Well, let's not worry about it right now. Hopefully, your mom will be okay, and you'll get a chance to clarify things with her."

"Oh, I will definitely want to do that," she said, turning to stare as the orderlies removed her mother from the emergency cubicle. She stared down at the small gray-haired lady as she was wheeled away, and said, "I can hardly believe it."

"Well, you should believe it," Melinda said. She turned and stormed from the ER.

Rosalina turned to look up at Gavin. "Could we get a DNA test, do you think?"

"I suggest we do," he said, studying her father on the bed, "because the repercussions are fairly major."

"I don't understand," she said. "What repercussions?"

"Let me check a few things first," he said. He gave her a hard kiss. "Stay here with your father, and I'll be back in a minute." She watched as he walked away, hating that he was even leaving her for a few moments. Because, in this world gone crazy, he was the one person she could trust.

GAVIN RACED OUTSIDE the main ER doors, grabbing his phone and having a short conversation with Lennox. "I know it's quite the bombshell," he said, "but it makes some sense."

"Maybe," he said, "but I'm not sure about that. We could run DNA. Get a swab from her, and I'll get the hospital to run swabs on both parents. But I don't know that we'll have access to any DNA on the grandfather, but the father's genes may be a half match for the grandfather's. Or something like that. It might be enough."

"I'll have to ask her about any mementos from her grandfather that may carry his genetic makeup. People save strands of hair from their babies, so maybe that happened with her grandfather, and Rosalina has that locket or whatever."

"Gavin, do you really think it's got something to do with

this?"

"It's the only thing that makes any sense," he said. "I've always thought it's been about the family. And that sister's a piece of work if I ever saw one. If there was ever a bigger bombshell than this, I don't know what it would be."

"Good point."

As he hung up with Lennox, Gavin turned to see Shane walking toward him. "Hey, did you find out anything?"

"You mean, besides the fact that you came racing to the hospital but not for me?" Shane asked.

"Obviously you got my text," Gavin said, "and things just blew up a little more." He quickly shared what Melinda had said.

"She's a real bitch, isn't she?" Shane said.

"Well, apparently she's done keeping secrets."

"She's still a bitch," he said. "It's pretty amazing, the web of secrets that people weave."

"Right? Amazing. Even after all we've seen."

"Now what do you want to do?" Shane asked his buddy.

"We need to get a DNA swab, so we can run some tests," Gavin said, "and see who else in this family has anything to do with this mess."

"I hear you there." As they walked back into the ER department, Shane asked, "How long will it take to run the test?"

"Well, if we get the military to do it, or get a special run on it, probably a week. But they'll have to bump a lot of other cases for it."

"Well, these lives are in danger," he said, "if we can't get some answers."

As soon as the guys stepped into the ER department, Gavin saw that the doctor had already been given orders and was taking a swab from Rosalina's mouth, in her parents' makeshift room, the curtain partially open.

She looked at him, her eyes wide and huge.

He joined her at the edge of the curtain. "It's the right thing to do right now," he said with a smile.

She nodded slowly. "I get that. I don't think I have any source of DNA from my grandfather though." Then she stopped and frowned. "Well, that's not true," she said. "I do have an old blanket of his."

"Well, if we need it, we might pull some hairs off it," he said, "but we might not have to."

"It still doesn't solve the problem of today."

He turned and looked to see that her father wasn't there. "Where's your father?"

"He's gone for an MRI," she said. "They should bring my mother back soon." She looked so lost and forlorn that he immediately wrapped her up in his arms again. She laid her head against his chest and just rested.

When he'd met her, she'd been so stiff and cold, but now she was anything but. He looked at Shane, who studied the change in their relationship with interest. Gavin gave a tiny shrug, as if to say, *It is what it is*, then he looked over the rest of the emergency room. "Hey, Shane, do you want to find Melinda?"

"I can do that," he said. "Or at least hopefully I can." He left and turned to look around. And heard a voice on the far side that was definitely Melinda's. "Sounds like she's at the front desk."

"Let's go talk to her," Rosalina said. As they headed down the hallway, they saw Steve and Melinda's children were there. She had the two kids, one by each hand, as she was talking to Steve. He looked at them and frowned immediately.

"You didn't have to leave her at the hotel," he protested.

"She didn't have to slam the elevator door in our faces in some childish attempt to get here first either," Rosalina said calmly. She looked at him and said, "Did you know?"

He had the grace to look ashamed, and he nodded. "Yes, I did."

"Interesting," Gavin said. "So, when are you guys getting married?"

They smiled and said, "We got married this morning," and held up rings on their fingers.

Rosalina stared at them in shock. "Why would you do that now?" she asked, puzzling it out.

But Gavin knew. "Oh, it's pretty easy to figure that one out," he said.

"Why is that?" Steve snapped.

"Because they weren't expecting your parents to survive, and they wanted to make sure they were legally married before such a time."

"So, this is all about inheritance?" Rosalina's voice rose. "No, Melinda. How could you?"

Melinda shrugged. "The company is mine now, you know."

"How do you figure?" Rosalina asked. "We each get half of their shares, and that's only if our parents don't survive."

"Well, that's as long as you were part of the will," she said, "but you can bet now that they've survived this scenario that I'll make sure that you aren't."

"Right," Gavin said, with a smile. "That's really what it's all about, isn't it, the company?"

"Of course it is. I'm the face of the company, and *she* can just butt out," Melinda said with a sneer.

But it wasn't Melinda's face Gavin was watching, it was Steve's.

Just then Shane stepped forward. "Well, I've done a little bit of research and contacted a few people too," he said.

Steve shrugged. "And?"

"At the moment we're doing a full search of your hotel room, your home stateside, and we've subpoenaed your phone records," he said with a smile.

Steve stiffened and glared at him. "What are you talking about?" he asked. "Why are you after me?"

"We just want to make sure that you had nothing to do with the attack on the family," Shane said.

"I didn't have anything to do with that," he said. "I came over here for a holiday. The parents knew we would get married here. We just didn't tell Rosalina about it."

"Why would you do that?" Rosalina cried out.

"Because I don't want you anywhere around us," Melinda said. "You are the foul result of an ugly affair."

"I'm still your blood," Rosalina snapped.

"Not my blood," she said, "and I won't have anything to do with *that woman* either."

"Your mother?" Shane asked.

"She's my father's wife," she said, "And that's as far as I'll go."

CHAPTER 14

ROSALINA COULDN'T QUITE understand all she heard. "Seriously, because she supposedly had an affair thirty years ago?"

"Because she had an affair and stuck us all with you," she said. "And then we have to consider who she had the affair with. That's just disgusting."

"And yet the woman isn't here to defend herself either," Gavin said. "And, of course, there'll be a full inquiry into this whole nightmare."

"Doesn't matter." Melinda and Steve both smiled.

Just then several cops came into the hospital, and Gavin motioned at the two. They immediately stepped up on either side of them.

"What's this all about?" Melinda asked. "Get away from me."

"Well, you're both under arrest," Gavin said smoothly. "For faking your kidnapping, for kidnapping your sister, and for kidnapping and hurting your parents."

"What are you talking about?" she sneered. "You don't have anything on us."

"Well, we'll see about that," Gavin said, studying Steve's face. "Did you really think it would be that easy?"

Steve glared at him but didn't say a word.

Rosalina stepped forward. "How did you know?" She

looked up at Gavin. "And why both of them?"

"It's why they got married," he said, "so they can't be compelled to testify against each other. Same reason Steve tied up Melinda—to throw us off from thinking they were the main culprits in all this mess."

Rosalina stopped, looked at Gavin in shock, and then turned to look at the other two and the smug expressions on their faces. "You beat up Mom and Dad and put them through all this, and then you thought you two wouldn't pay for it?"

"We didn't do anything," Steve said.

"Besides, what difference does it make?" Melinda sneered.

"You tell me?" Rosalina said, obviously still confused. "Why would you do it? I don't understand the motivation."

"Because it's time for them to retire," Melinda said. "They were giving me a lot of guff and threatened to change the will," she said. "So I had to show them who had the upper hand."

Rosalina stared in shock at the petulant and ever-childlike personality of her sister, who thought she should have whatever she wanted, regardless of the cost. Rosalina was silent for a few moments as she took it all in. "You actually hired like a dozen people to kidnap us, to take Mom and Dad away, and to put us in a basement, where you were gagged and I wasn't, which I didn't quite understand. And then have our parents beaten up?"

"We didn't have them beaten up," she sneered again. "We beat them up ourselves. They needed a little convincing. But we have the will, and it's been changed."

"It won't matter in the least," Shane said with a smile.

Melinda glared at him. "What are you talking about?"

"Well," Shane began, "that will was coerced from your parents, while under duress. Makes it invalid. And the hospital has the medical records to prove they were forced to change their wills, plus the word of your own parents, who remain alive despite your attempts otherwise. Yet the more pressing document is your grandfather's will—"

"What?" Melinda screamed.

Shane smiled at her with glee. "And I've already talked to the lawyer. That will states that the grandfather's stock ownership in the company was to be given to *all* offspring, not just your father, which was his only offspring at the time this will was drawn.

"Your father's name is mentioned therein, but, since the will states *given to all offspring*, and—as you've so helpfully pointed out, Melinda, that your sister Rosalina is also your grandfather's daughter—so she and your father each get half of your grandfather's trust, to be released in two days' time per his will.

"At that time, per my math, your father will be the major shareholder with 30 percent of the shares. Then Rosalina with her 23.5 percent. Then your mother, with 16.5 percent. That leaves you, Melinda, with your 10 percent still and the few smaller shareholders. But"—Shane stopped Melinda from interrupting with a raised finger—"don't forget that Rosalina will also get her part of your mother's shares when she passes on—hopefully not to happen for many years from now, and let's pray it is a natural passing. So your dad and Rosalina are the major shareholders now in the entire corporation," Shane said smoothly, "even without Rosalina having her mother's shares."

"*Nooo*," Melinda screamed. "You lie!"

"Actually there's more, Melinda. So listen up," Shane

said, his smile huge this whole time. "The lawyer is looking into various legalities, but it seems when your father passes, his stock may go to Rosalina as well."

"No, no, no!"

"Since he was legally married to your mother at the time she gave birth to Rosalina, some jurisdictions deem the husband the legal father of any child born of the marriage, regardless of DNA findings."

"No, no, no!" Melinda added a foot stomp for good measure, thrashing her arms around.

"Oh, but you haven't heard the best part yet, Melinda." Shane smiled.

"Well, get on with it, you idiot."

"I believe, since you are going to jail, you forfeit your right to any inheritance."

"Nooooooo! No. No! You lie!"

"Plus just think what your parents may decide to do about the 10 percent share you own now, after what you did to them."

Melinda yelled, "It was all Steve!"

At that, the cops stepped forward and grabbed the couple and took them away. Melinda was screaming back at them, "You can't do this! I have to stay and look after my children."

Around the corner walked the two children, who looked at Rosalina. "Are you doing this to our mommy?"

She crouched beside them and whispered, "No, and you'll see them after their lawyers get here." They nodded, and their nanny came around the corner just then, and they ran to her.

Rosalina looked up at the nanny. "I didn't even realize you were here with them," she said apologetically.

The nanny frowned. "But that's the way they like it, isn't it?" she asked. "I'll take the children back to the hotel. When there is an opportunity, could somebody please let me know what we're supposed to do?" And, with that, she ushered the children from the hospital.

"You didn't know the nanny was here?" Gavin asked her.

Rosalina shook her head. "I hadn't seen her since we arrived in Hawaii."

"Does she travel with them often?"

She nodded. "She's been with them since the children were young," she said.

"Interesting," Gavin said, looping an arm around her shoulder and tucking her up close. "So, what would you like to do now?"

"I'd like to stay with my parents," she said, "at least for a while."

"You're hoping your mom wakes up?" he asked.

She smiled and nodded. "I'd like to ask her a few questions." She looked at Shane. "Did you mean it?"

He nodded. "Yes, while you've been in here, we've been making a lot of phone calls. Obviously DNA tests need to be done to confirm your position in the company," he said, "but your grandfather's will was very clear that it was to be left to *all* offspring. And that's a fairly common wording, depending on how early in life the will is made. You'd never want to cut out another offspring by only naming one, the firstborn of many."

"And do you think Dad knew?"

"I have no idea."

Gavin said, "But I highly suggest it's time for the secrets to stop and for the truth to come out."

Just then the doctor called out to Rosalina. She raced over, and her mother was back again in her temporary cubicle, but this time with her eyes open. She looked up at Rosalina and immediately started to cry. Rosalina bent over to give her a hug. "It's okay, Mom. You're safe now."

She shook her head. "No, we're never safe," she said, "It's your sister. Melinda did this to us."

"I get that now," she said. "She's been taken away by the police."

Her mother looked at her, and a sigh of relief came out. "It's been such a nightmare."

"Apparently a thirty-year-long nightmare," Rosalina said, smiling down at the woman who gave birth to her. "Sounds like we have a lot to talk about."

Her mother's eyes filled with tears. "Oh, can you ever forgive me?"

"It's not for me to judge," Rosalina said gently. "I'm just so happy that you're okay."

"Maybe not when you hear all the details," she said.

Rosalina leaned over, kissed the frail woman on the cheek, and whispered, "I promise that I'll still love you anyway."

Her mother's eyes filled with tears, and she promised that she'd answer all of Rosalina's questions.

She could feel Gavin's hand on her shoulder as he drew her just outside her mom's cubicle.

He whispered, "You're a really special person, you know that?"

"She's been through enough," Rosalina said. "I'm afraid my sister has been blackmailing her for all these years. If that's even partly true, she's suffered plenty."

"And you?"

"I guess it made me who I am," she said thoughtfully. "Besides, my parents aren't all that old, and, while the first thirty years were rough, maybe the next thirty can be a whole lot better. And I was blessed. I had my grandparents back then. And now I have you. If you'll stick around, that is?"

He looked down at their interlaced fingers and whispered, "I don't see how I can't. I've never met anybody quite like you, and I don't want to experience life without you at my side."

She squeezed his fingers gently and looked back at her mom to see her tears slowing down. Stepping inside the cubicle again, she leaned down and whispered, "Rest, Mom. It'll be okay. I promise. Just rest."

Holding her mother's hand in one of hers and Gavin's hand in her other, Rosalina took a deep breath, realizing that finally, after all this time, life had the potential to be pretty damn good.

EPILOGUE

SHANE ANDREWS OPENED his apartment door, walked inside, and tossed his duffel bag down. He headed to the fridge, pulled out a cold beer, and stepped out on his small deck. He popped the top and took a long cold drink. That had been one hell of a job in Hawaii. But a lot of healing needed to happen now for that family. Not only did the parents have to heal but the children and the grandchildren were involved as well. He didn't understand somebody being so self-centered, so selfish as Melinda that she would put her parents and her sister through so much just to make sure Melinda got what she wanted.

Melinda had been a piece of work. That she'd always been a suspect right from the beginning didn't surprise him, just because her attitude had been so off. But to find out that Steve, a member of the navy, a guy he should have been able to trust, had been a willing party to it all filled Shane with horror.

He rotated his neck, trying to stretch out some of the kinks. It had been a long two days. He was home now and needed a few days' break. At least he hoped he got a couple days off. He'd taken an extra day to stay with the family and Gavin over there to tie up things and to get all the facts straight.

But now that Shane was home, he threw himself onto

the lounge chair and relaxed. He didn't know quite what the next few days would bring, but he was up for it. At least he thought he would be. It was a hell of a deal joining the Mavericks, but he was pretty happy with his decision. If ever somebody needed to be stopped, it was Melinda. He hadn't expected this to be the level of the work he would be doing. Still, it was what it was. As he sat here, his phone buzzed, and he smiled when he saw it was Gavin. He hit the Talk button. "I'm home, safe and sound, bud. No need to worry about me."

"Hey, I just wanted to make sure you were looking after that leg of yours," he said.

"Yep, we're all good."

"Good," he said. "How do you feel about New York?"

"Why the hell would I want to go there?" he asked.

At that, Gavin laughed. "Remember Diesel?"

"Diesel Edwards? Yeah, I remember. What about him?"

"He'll be waiting for you there at the airport."

"Shit, am I leaving already?" Shane asked, as he looked at his beer.

"Absolutely. Well, you're leaving in about three hours," he said.

"Wow, not even enough time to do a load of laundry."

"Sure there is, if you put down that beer, get up off your ass, and get your clothes in the machine," Gavin said, laughing. "You can drink it while they wash."

"What am I doing in New York?" he asked, as he walked back to his bag of dirty clothes and did exactly that. With the washing machine started, he grabbed his beer and looked down at his phone. "So, what aren't you saying?"

"It looks like a hostage situation has gone down in a big telecom building," he said.

"What's that got to do with me?"

"Well, Diesel is already in position or will be. He'll pick you up at the airport. You are going into the tunnels and coming up through the basement."

"What the hell does SWAT have to say about that?"

"Well, they're hoping this might be right up your alley."

"Why is that?"

"Because, uh, … because one of your best friends is in there."

At that moment, everything inside Shane froze.

"Shelly?" He remembered her saying she had a brand-new job in New York. "I know she lives there, but what's she doing in the telecom building?"

"She was a new hire about forty-five days ago," he said. "Didn't you hear about it?"

And, of course, he had, but he had completely forgotten. "So why do you think she's involved? That's a huge building."

"Because the kidnappers said she was. And they are hanging on to her until you arrive. So get yourself ready and get out there."

This concludes Book 11 of The Mavericks: Gavin.

Read about Shane: The Mavericks, Book 11

The Mavericks: Gavin (Book #12)

What happens when the very men—trained to make the hard decisions—come up against the rules and regulations that hold them back from doing what needs to be done? They either stay and work within the constraints given to them or they walk away. Only now, for a select few, they have another option:

The Mavericks. A covert black ops team that steps up and break all the rules … but gets the job done.

Welcome to a new military romance series by *USA Today* best-selling author Dale Mayer. A series where you meet new friends and just might get to meet old ones too in this raw and compelling look at the men who keep us safe every day from the darkness where they operate—and live—in the shadows … until someone special helps them step into the light.

Her kidnappers demanded Shane arrive. Finding out his best friend was held as a pawn just pissed him off. Finding out rescuing her was a test made him seriously angry. He hates being used. These men mean business though, as Shane finds a body count too high for comfort.

Shelly knew Shane would come for her. No way he wouldn't. She was lucky to have Shane there for her, especially when learning a second woman had been kidnapped and held for over six months. The simple rescue of Shelly turns into something more to find this second woman.

But is there one killer boss out there or two? As the pair try to secure their own freedom, it gets even murkier, until finding a way through is paramount. Otherwise no one gets a happy ending.

Find book 12 here!
To find out more visit Dale Mayer's website.
http://smarturl.it/DMSShane

Author's Note

Thank you for reading Gavin: The Mavericks, Book 11! If you enjoyed the book, please take a moment and leave a short review.

Dear reader,

I love to hear from readers, and you can contact me at my website: www.dalemayer.com or at my Facebook author page. To be informed of new releases and special offers, sign up for my newsletter or follow me on BookBub. And if you are interested in joining Dale Mayer's Reader Group, here is the Facebook sign up page.
https://smarturl.it/DaleMayerFBGroup

Cheers,
Dale Mayer

Get THREE Free Books Now!

Have you met the SEALS of Honor?

SEALs of Honor Books 1, 2, and 3. Follow the stories of brave, badass warriors who serve their country with honor and love their women to the limits of life and death.

Read Mason, Hawk, and Dane right now for FREE.

Go here and tell me where to send them!
http://smarturl.it/EthanBofB

About the Author

Dale Mayer is a USA Today bestselling author best known for her Psychic Visions and Family Blood Ties series. Her contemporary romances are raw and full of passion and emotion (Second Chances, SKIN), her thrillers will keep you guessing (By Death series), and her romantic comedies will keep you giggling (It's a Dog's Life and Charmin Marvin Romantic Comedy series).

She honors the stories that come to her – and some of them are crazy and break all the rules and cross multiple genres!

To go with her fiction, she also writes nonfiction in many different fields with books available on resume writing, companion gardening and the US mortgage system. She has recently published her Career Essentials Series. All her books are available in print and ebook format.

Connect with Dale Mayer Online

Dale's Website – www.dalemayer.com
Facebook Personal – https://smarturl.it/DaleMayerFacebook
Instagram – https://smarturl.it/DaleMayerInstagram
BookBub – https://smarturl.it/DaleMayerBookbub
Facebook Fan Page – https://smarturl.it/DaleMayerFBFanPage
Goodreads – https://smarturl.it/DaleMayerGoodreads

Also by Dale Mayer

Published Adult Books:

Hathaway House
Aaron, Book 1

Brock, Book 2

Cole, Book 3

Denton, Book 4

Elliot, Book 5

Finn, Book 6

Gregory, Book 7

Heath, Book 8

Iain, Book 9

Jaden, Book 10

Keith, Book 11

Lance, Book 12

Melissa, Book 13

Nash, Book 14

Owen, Book 15

Hathaway House, Books 1–3

Hathaway House, Books 4–6

Hathaway House, Books 7–9

The K9 Files
Ethan, Book 1

Pierce, Book 2

Zane, Book 3

Blaze, Book 4
Lucas, Book 5
Parker, Book 6
Carter, Book 7
Weston, Book 8
Greyson, Book 9
Rowan, Book 10
Caleb, Book 11

Lovely Lethal Gardens

Arsenic in the Azaleas, Book 1
Bones in the Begonias, Book 2
Corpse in the Carnations, Book 3
Daggers in the Dahlias, Book 4
Evidence in the Echinacea, Book 5
Footprints in the Ferns, Book 6
Gun in the Gardenias, Book 7
Handcuffs in the Heather, Book 8
Ice Pick in the Ivy, Book 9
Jewels in the Juniper, Book 10
Killer in the Kiwis, Book 11
Lovely Lethal Gardens, Books 1–2
Lovely Lethal Gardens, Books 3–4
Lovely Lethal Gardens, Books 5–6

Psychic Vision Series

Tuesday's Child
Hide 'n Go Seek
Maddy's Floor
Garden of Sorrow
Knock Knock…
Rare Find
Eyes to the Soul

Now You See Her
Shattered
Into the Abyss
Seeds of Malice
Eye of the Falcon
Itsy-Bitsy Spider
Unmasked
Deep Beneath
From the Ashes
Stroke of Death
Ice Maiden
Psychic Visions Books 1–3
Psychic Visions Books 4–6
Psychic Visions Books 7–9

By Death Series
Touched by Death
Haunted by Death
Chilled by Death
By Death Books 1–3

Broken Protocols – Romantic Comedy Series
Cat's Meow
Cat's Pajamas
Cat's Cradle
Cat's Claus
Broken Protocols 1-4

Broken and... Mending
Skin
Scars
Scales (of Justice)
Broken but... Mending 1-3

Glory

Genesis

Tori

Celeste

Glory Trilogy

Biker Blues

Morgan: Biker Blues, Volume 1

Cash: Biker Blues, Volume 2

SEALs of Honor

Mason: SEALs of Honor, Book 1

Hawk: SEALs of Honor, Book 2

Dane: SEALs of Honor, Book 3

Swede: SEALs of Honor, Book 4

Shadow: SEALs of Honor, Book 5

Cooper: SEALs of Honor, Book 6

Markus: SEALs of Honor, Book 7

Evan: SEALs of Honor, Book 8

Mason's Wish: SEALs of Honor, Book 9

Chase: SEALs of Honor, Book 10

Brett: SEALs of Honor, Book 11

Devlin: SEALs of Honor, Book 12

Easton: SEALs of Honor, Book 13

Ryder: SEALs of Honor, Book 14

Macklin: SEALs of Honor, Book 15

Corey: SEALs of Honor, Book 16

Warrick: SEALs of Honor, Book 17

Tanner: SEALs of Honor, Book 18

Jackson: SEALs of Honor, Book 19

Kanen: SEALs of Honor, Book 20

Nelson: SEALs of Honor, Book 21

Taylor: SEALs of Honor, Book 22

Colton: SEALs of Honor, Book 23

Troy: SEALs of Honor, Book 24

Axel: SEALs of Honor, Book 25

SEALs of Honor, Books 1–3

SEALs of Honor, Books 4–6

SEALs of Honor, Books 7–10

SEALs of Honor, Books 11–13

SEALs of Honor, Books 14–16

SEALs of Honor, Books 17–19

SEALs of Honor, Books 20–22

Heroes for Hire

Levi's Legend: Heroes for Hire, Book 1

Stone's Surrender: Heroes for Hire, Book 2

Merk's Mistake: Heroes for Hire, Book 3

Rhodes's Reward: Heroes for Hire, Book 4

Flynn's Firecracker: Heroes for Hire, Book 5

Logan's Light: Heroes for Hire, Book 6

Harrison's Heart: Heroes for Hire, Book 7

Saul's Sweetheart: Heroes for Hire, Book 8

Dakota's Delight: Heroes for Hire, Book 9

Michael's Mercy (Part of Sleeper SEAL Series)

Tyson's Treasure: Heroes for Hire, Book 10

Jace's Jewel: Heroes for Hire, Book 11

Rory's Rose: Heroes for Hire, Book 12

Brandon's Bliss: Heroes for Hire, Book 13

Liam's Lily: Heroes for Hire, Book 14

North's Nikki: Heroes for Hire, Book 15

Anders's Angel: Heroes for Hire, Book 16

Reyes's Raina: Heroes for Hire, Book 17

Dezi's Diamond: Heroes for Hire, Book 18

Vince's Vixen: Heroes for Hire, Book 19

Ice's Icing: Heroes for Hire, Book 20
Johan's Joy: Heroes for Hire, Book 21
Galen's Gemma: Heroes for Hire, Book 22
Zack's Zest: Heroes for Hire, Book 23
Heroes for Hire, Books 1–3
Heroes for Hire, Books 4–6
Heroes for Hire, Books 7–9
Heroes for Hire, Books 10–12
Heroes for Hire, Books 13–15

SEALs of Steel
Badger: SEALs of Steel, Book 1
Erick: SEALs of Steel, Book 2
Cade: SEALs of Steel, Book 3
Talon: SEALs of Steel, Book 4
Laszlo: SEALs of Steel, Book 5
Geir: SEALs of Steel, Book 6
Jager: SEALs of Steel, Book 7
The Final Reveal: SEALs of Steel, Book 8
SEALs of Steel, Books 1–4
SEALs of Steel, Books 5–8
SEALs of Steel, Books 1–8

The Mavericks
Kerrick, Book 1
Griffin, Book 2
Jax, Book 3
Beau, Book 4
Asher, Book 5
Ryker, Book 6
Miles, Book 7
Nico, Book 8
Keane, Book 9

Lennox, Book 10

Gavin, Book 11

Shane, Book 12

Bullard's Battle Series

Ryland's Reach, Book 1

Cain's Cross, Book 2

Eton's Escape, Book 3

Garret's Gambit, Book 4

Kano's Keep, Book 5

Fallon's Flaw, Book 6

Quinn's Quest, Book 7

Bullard's Beauty, Book 8

Collections

Dare to Be You…

Dare to Love…

Dare to be Strong…

RomanceX3

Standalone Novellas

It's a Dog's Life

Riana's Revenge

Second Chances

Published Young Adult Books:

Family Blood Ties Series

Vampire in Denial

Vampire in Distress

Vampire in Design

Vampire in Deceit

Vampire in Defiance

Vampire in Conflict
Vampire in Chaos
Vampire in Crisis
Vampire in Control
Vampire in Charge
Family Blood Ties Set 1–3
Family Blood Ties Set 1–5
Family Blood Ties Set 4–6
Family Blood Ties Set 7–9
Sian's Solution, A Family Blood Ties Series Prequel
    Novelette

Design series
Dangerous Designs
Deadly Designs
Darkest Designs
Design Series Trilogy

Standalone
In Cassie's Corner
Gem Stone (a Gemma Stone Mystery)
Time Thieves

Published Non-Fiction Books:

Career Essentials
Career Essentials: The Résumé
Career Essentials: The Cover Letter
Career Essentials: The Interview
Career Essentials: 3 in 1